Coley blanched at Jase's words, but didn't answer. Suddenly her face was caught in his hands and twisted fiercely up toward him. "Yes, they did," she whispered. Tears blurred her vision. "It doesn't matter."

Jase laughed cynically. "It does matter. If anyone saw us together they'd probably forbid me to set foot on this land again."

Coley was crying openly now. "This land! That's all you care about." Bitterness entered her voice. "You'd kill for this land!" Silence fell as the full horror and unspeakable cruelty of her words dawned on her. "I didn't mean it, Jase—"

He turned and walked away into the darkness. And Coley realized that nothing she could do or say would bring him back to her now....

JANET DAILEY AMERICANA

SAVAGE LAND

Harlequin Books

TORONTO • NEW YORK • LONDON
AMSTERDAM • PARIS • SYDNEY • HAMBURG
STOCKHOLM • ATHENS • TOKYO • MILAN
MADRID • WARSAW • BUDAPEST • AUCKLAND

The state flower depicted on the cover of this book is bluebonnet.

Janet Dailey Americana edition published March 1988
Second printing October 1988
Third printing October 1989
Fourth printing October 1990
Fifth printing December 1991
Sixth printing September 1992
Seventh printing November 1992

ISBN 0-373-89893-2

Harlequin Presents edition published May 1976
Second printing September 1977
Third printing March 1979
Fourth printing April 1981

Original hardcover edition published in 1974
by Mills & Boon Limited

SAVAGE LAND

CHAPTER ONE

ANOTHER bolt of lightning flamed out of the dark, rolling clouds, followed by a heart-pounding clap of thunder. Colleen McGuire's pulse raced as she involuntarily cringed in her seat. Her large hazel eyes remained fixed on the windshield where the wipers were vainly attempting to wash away the sheets of rain descending from the menacing clouds. Apprehensively she glanced at her brother behind the wheel.

'Danny, don't you think we should stop?' Fear brought a trembling to her words in spite of her effort to control it.

'Just where would you suggest, Coley?' he snapped, not taking his attention from the emptiness in front of them. 'If we stop now, we probably won't get this old clunker started again.'

'We should have listened to that man back at the garage,' Coley murmured as a fresh torrent of water pummelled down on their car.

'That was thirty miles back, and it was only sprinkling then!' Danny flashed at her. Tension from the strain of creeping along the winding Texas road made him unnaturally sharp. 'How was I supposed to know it would be like this!'

'But he said it was raining bad in the mountains, that the road could flood. And those signs we've been seeing,' Coley persisted logically. At her words, a highway sign was illuminated by their car's headlights—'During wet weather, watch low water crossings'. A sickening moan escaped her lips. 'Oh, Danny, there's another!'

'Coley, will you stop carrying on about a little rain and thunder! Aren't you ever going to grow out of that childish fear?' her brother retorted. His knuckles were white from gripping the steering wheel as if his life depended on him not letting it go. With determination, he added, 'We're going to make it. Don't you worry.'

A forced smile appeared on Coley's mouth as she gulped down her fears and turned to look out her side window. Instinctively her long fingers went to her mouth, where she absently chewed on a nail while watching the jagged forks of lightning turn the hills and mountains around them into towering monsters. Her reflection in the window glass dimly mirrored her thin, angular face with its fine, arched brows, and large hazel eyes that had, if it was possible, grown wider with her anxiety, and her button nose that was fogging a small section of the glass. Her wispy brown hair was as indistinct in the reflection as it was in life, limply hanging below her gamin ears. And yet there was a childlike charm about her that was oddly appealing and a promise of unusual beauty at maturity.

The old Chevy slowed slightly while water swirled around its wheels. It was another water crossing. The colour washed out of Coley's face as she turned her head from the sickening rush of the stream. Numbly she watched her brother's taut face, feeling the current tugging at the car, trying to sweep it off the road. Coley felt herself stiffen with Danny as they slowly edged their way between two poles midway in the crossing. The water was above the hubcaps and inching under the door before they finally made it to the other side. Coley could see the relief on her brother's face when they reached solid ground again.

'What were those poles there for?' She forced herself to speak to stem the rising panic within her, knowing her brother was beginning to worry, too. When he failed to answer her immediately, she repeated the question.

'High water markers,' he replied grimly. His young face was beginning to show the strain of the constant demands on his driving ability. He glanced worriedly over at his sister before returning to the road. 'I'm sure we don't have too much farther to go.'

Despite his attempt to reassure her, his growing apprehension increased her fear. Danny was ten months younger than she, but he had always taken the part of 'older brother', watching over and protecting Coley even now when she was almost twenty.

'I wish we would have let Aunt Wilhelmina know we were coming.' Coley's eyes ruefully surveyed the lonely stretch ahead where canyons poked shadowy fingers at the road. 'At least someone would know we were here. Why didn't you let me write and tell her we were coming?'

A cynical laugh slipped out of Danny's drawn lips. But he couldn't voice his feelings because he knew his soft-hearted sister didn't realize that people often extended offers of help with no intentions of having them accepted. Never having met Aunt Wilhelmina, he had deliberately not notified her for fear that she would retract her invitation for them to come live with her.

Hesitantly he glanced over at Coley huddled on the passenger seat flinching at each crash of lightning.

Silently he studied her long-limbed body and the cheap flowered print dress she wore before grimly turning back to stare out the rain-coated windshield. 'What a rotten life she's had,' he thought, not considering that his had been the same. The first time that he had recognized and understood the abuse they had received at the hands of their father was during one of his drunks, when Danny had done his best to shield his sister and to protect her if he 'could. Sober, their father had been a wonderful man, but he hadn't been sober very often. There had been a subconscious relief when he had finally been killed in a car wreck—the result of drunken driving.

But for Danny and Coley in the first years of their teens, the hardships had just begun. Their mother, delicate all her life, within a year was an invalid from asthma. It was shortly after that that a stubborn pride and hardened bitterness grew in Danny, not for the luxuries they were deprived of, nor the constant part-time jobs that he took to earn enough money to keep them going, but for the clucking tongues of neighbours that continuously deplored their lack of supervision out of one side of their mouths while offering empty promises of help at the same time.

Their mother had refused to let either of them leave school, which Danny supposed he should be grateful for. But since both he and Coley had to rush away as soon as the last bell rang, he to go to work and Coley to look after their mother, there had never been any time for sports, or school dances, or friends. He didn't mind, because 'men' didn't miss those things, but Coley should have had them instead of housework, cooking and nursing.

'Why do you suppose Momma never mentioned

Aunt Wilhelmina?' A frown creased Coley's wide forehead, unknowingly interrupting Danny's musings.

'I don't know,' Danny shrugged. 'I'm just glad she had an aunt.'

'Aren't you just the teensiest bit scared? Coming out here and presenting yourself to a complete stranger who didn't even know we existed until you wrote her that letter telling her Mother had died.'

Coley had never been around other people much and strangers tended to make her shy and withdrawn. Her quiet ways usually made people forget she was there, which increased her reserve. Almost hypnotized by the back and forth sweep of the wipers, she remembered the day he had been helping Danny go through their mother's trunk about a week after the funeral. Coley hadn't quite understood his excitement at finding that letter at the bottom of a pile of old photographs. With painstaking care he had written this unknown relative, saying a silent prayer that she hadn't died already. When the reply and invitation came just a week ago, Danny had walked into the restaurant where Coley had a job as waitress and, with a jubilant air of satisfaction, told her to quit. How he had hated her working there and the off-colour remarks his naïve 'little' sister was subjected to. He didn't like the idea that Coley, marked for future beauty in his eyes, should lower herself to serving people who weren't fit to serve her. His conviction had deepened when he had caught Carl making a pass at Coley.

Another roll of thunder reverberated out of the hills, drawing a terrified gasp from Coley. Glancing over at her tightly clasped yet trembling fists, Danny fortified his confidence in his decision.

'We've got to forget everything we've left behind us,' he said. 'This is our chance to start a whole new life, to make something of ourselves with nobody around to tell us we can't do it.'

'But we could have done that in San Antoine,' she replied, gazing earnestly at her brother. 'With me working, we would have had enough money to get a nicer apartment, and later I could have got a better job. And you had so many friends there.'

'I couldn't stand you working in that place,' he declared vehemently. 'And the thought of you marrying one of those "friends" and having a bunch of squalling brats running around makes me sick. No, when you marry, it's going to be somebody respectable who can give you your own home and nice clothes. He's going to be good and decent, not someone like Carl.'

A shudder quaked through Coley as the repulsive memory swept through her. How she had tried to forget that night when Carl had taken her home, saying that Danny was going to be late. She had tried to be polite despite her inner revulsion of him, because he was Danny's friend. She could still remember the way his dark eyes had raked over her as he unlocked the apartment door and barred her entry with a tanned arm. Numbly she had stood silent, a crimson blush covering her face. She could still hear his mocking laugh as he teased her about her unkissed lips before slipping a slender arm behind her back and drawing her to him. She had tried to push herself away from him, but he had only laughed and forced her face to his. The naked lust in his face had terrified her, but she had been helpless against his animal strength. The opportune arrival of Danny and his strident yell broke the one-sided embrace. In a tightly controlled temper,

10

her brother ordered Carl out, but not before he had winked cockily at Coley.

A fresh onslaught of rain stirred Coley out of her reflection. Silently she watched the headlight beams pick out another water crossing ahead of them. The angry black water swirled menacingly before them as she felt Danny change gears in anticipation. Again in the middle of the crossing were markers with water churning below the three foot mark.

'Danny, it's too deep!' she cried. 'We'll never make it across!'

Her brother's face was ashen as they inched their way through the water. Her breathing stopped while the swift current swayed the back end. They were almost on the other side when the motor died. Gasping, Coley turned her terrified eyes to Danny and watched him vainly attempt to start it again. It was no use. The dull hum of the starter foretold the futility despite earnest pleadings from the driver. In a fit of anger, Danny jerked the key out of the ignition and looked at Coley sitting petrified on the opposite side of the car.

'I'm sorry, Coley,' he muttered. 'We'll have to leave the car. Let me get out my side first.'

Rolling down his window, Danny squirmed out the narrow opening into the swirling dark waters. Coley watched him make his way through the driving rain around to her side. Storms had always terrified her and being stranded afoot in one of such violence sent an earthquake through her body. Bravely she crawled through her window to Danny's waiting arms.

'I can walk,' she protested faintly when Danny continued carrying her until they were out of the stream. Watching the rain stream down his troubled face as he stood her up, she added, 'I'm all right, Danny. I can make it.'

He smiled proudly at her already rain-soaked head inches below his before searching the cloud-darkened countryside. His gaze stopped at the faint outline of a plateau with an overhanging section of rock.

Pointing towards it, he instructed, 'Do you see that place where the rocks jut out over that high area? I want you to go there and wait for me. I saw a lane back on the other side and it might lead to a house and help.'

'No, Danny, let me come with you,' Coley cried. 'I'm not a child. I can make it.'

'There's no sense in both of us going,' he replied. 'I'll come back for you just as soon as I can.'

He didn't give her any further opportunity to protest, but immediately waded into the swollen waters of the crossing. Coley stretched out her arm to him, then drew it back to cover her mouth as she watched him disappear into the flooding waters. He was swimming now as a glimpse of his white face appeared to her in the midst of another flash of lightning. The swift, churning current dragged him downstream, but her impatient eyes saw him reach the other side and struggle on to the bank. Gratefully, Coley saw him wave that he was okay and cup his hands to call to her, but his voice was carried away by the thunder. He was probably reassuring her that he would be back, and she waved in answer. Then he was gone, swallowed up in the blackness of the land.

Silently she stood watching the empty road until a bolt of lightning crashed again to the ground, jolting her out of her immobility. Conscious of her sodden dress and the chilling cold creeping into her bones. Coley struck out for the shelter Danny had pointed out to her. It looked farther away now than it did before and she cast a rueful glance down at her sandals as she set out. Determined not to lose her way, she picked out landmarks, a yucca plant here, farther on a willow, all in a straight line with her destination. Her long legs doggedly placed one foot in front of the other ignoring the slippery, muddy ground.

Four times Coley stopped and wiped the rain from her face to peer through the sheets of water at her goal. Panting now with the cold beginning to chatter her teeth, she pushed on until she reached the bottom of the hill. The slope up was a lot steeper than it looked. With water oozing out of the spongy ground, she knew she would have to crawl up the hill. Coley gazed back forlornly to the road, but her vision was obscured twenty feet around her by the rain. She couldn't even see the top of the hill except when the lightning illuminated the sky with its eerie forked tongue. Sighing her despair, she turned to the hill.

If only she could have gone with Danny, she thought, but she knew she would never have made it across. She couldn't swim.

The slick-soled sandals couldn't find a foothold in the slimy hill, reducing Coley to clawing her way with her hands and pushing herself up with her knees. Her new nylons were in shreds and her best dress stained with mud. Her breath came in panic-born sobs as she fought to keep herself from sliding back. She was almost at the top. Gasping in the rain-laden air, she dug her long fingers into the ground to pull herself closer.

A hand grabbed hold of her arm; another caught her under the opposite shoulder and she was on top! A faint laugh escaped between her gasps for breath as Coley took a muddy hand to wipe the hair out of her face. 'Danny made it. He's already here,' her thoughts cried.

'Oh, Danny!' she sobbed aloud, just as a silver-gold tongue of lightning licked a nearby hill. The words froze in her throat. Standing before her was a tall, dark form with a cape billowing sinisterly about him, a hat pulled low on his face, but not so low that Coley couldn't see the short stubble of a dark beard and the haunting hollows of his eyes during that brief flash. Behind him loomed a shiny black horse, his head tossing and his hooves pawing viciously at the ground.

Recovering her wits, Coley managed to stammer, 'My br-brother went ... our car....'

'I saw it,' was the abrupt reply. His voice was deep and sharp.

Coley watched in petrified silence as the stranger swung into the saddle. Was he going to leave her? Nudging the prancing horse over beside her, he lowered a shiny-coated arm to her. Frightened, she started to step back.

'Come on!' Impatience growled through his words. 'We can't stay in the rain all night.'

He didn't really expect her to get on that horse, she thought. She'd never been on a horse in her life! But common sense had moved her hand into his and she was effortlessly swung up in front of him.

'W-where are we going?' stuttered Coley as he tucked the front of his rain slicker, that she had thought a cape, around her to afford her as much protection as was possible from the downpour.

'There's an old lineshack on the other side of the hill,' he replied, an arm holding her slight, boyish figure closely to him. He nudged his horse into a walk and despite the strength of his arm, Coley felt her

14

perch, so high off the ground, rather precarious especially with the rolling motion of the horse's shoulders.

The warmth of the stranger's body slowly seeped into her, though she shivered helplessly in her wet dress. His broad shoulders dwarfed her with their immensity and her rain-soaked brown hair felt the occasional brush of hair from his unshaven chin. Coley's heart pounded wildly at the closeness of the forbidding stranger, compounded by the violent storm that turned the most innocent objects into sinister shapes. The splintering crashes of lightning, the death drums of the thunder and the rhythmic slush-slushing of the horse's hooves were the only sounds to accompany the rainfall.

'What—what are you doing out here?' Coley finally asked, almost suffocated by the quietness of her rescuer.

'Looking for dumb animals.' His reply was sarcastic and sharp.

A spark of indignation flamed briefly in Coley before she asserted, 'My brother went to get help. He'll be back soon with someone to help him pull the car out and get it started.'

'Not in this weather he won't,' his voice growled just above her ear. 'Besides, I saw your car floating away just before I saw you. The water's too high now for any kind of travelling, so wherever your brother went, he's stranded for the night the same as we are.'

Through the gruffness and censure of his voice, Coley recognized an educated tone and considered her companion in a new light. She started to speak again, but stopped when the looming outline of a building appeared before them. Halting his mount in front of the gloomy shack, the man lowered Coley to the ground before he dismounted to nestle her under the crook of his arm, his slicker an umbrella over her head. He half carried her beneath the overhang where he stopped and put a shoulder to the swollen door. Grudgingly it opened, yawning its blackness in their face. Hesitantly, Coley followed the impatient beckoning of his hand into the void. Her bright, wondering eyes peered uselessly around as she clutched her arms tightly about her, while the stranger walked directly to his left where the scrape of a match gave birth to a light. It flickered dimly for a moment inside the chimney of a lantern before spreading its cheerful rays to all but the darkest corners of the room. Coley watched numbly as the lantern was carried over to rest near the centre of the room. Without wasting motion, the stranger knelt before the fireplace and after the first crackle of flame devouring paper, began adding wood from a nearby box. As soon as it was sufficiently started not to require his attention, he turned to a makeshift bed near the fire, pulled off a blanket and tossed it to the girl shivering before him.

'Get those wet things off and wrap yourself in this,' he ordered before walking to the door.

'Where are you going?' Coley gasped, detaining his arm with her hand.

The searching probes of light sifted through the shadows on his face revealing the previously hidden features. Her eyes widened as she saw the jagged scar across his left cheek. Startled, her gaze flew to his eyes to find that the dark shadows of the storm had hidden two piercing blue diamonds now gleaming down on her with their coldness. In a trance she noted his nostrils swell in anger before the grim mouth opened to reply to her question. She swiftly withdrew her hand from his arm, knowing her expression must mirror her surprise and horror.

'I'm going to take care of the horse,' he snapped.

'I'm sorry,' Coley murmured, ashamed of her unspeakable cruelty when she let him see her shock at his disfigurement, but the door had already slammed shut.

Glumly Coley turned back towards the fire, idly twiddling with the blanket. That was a rotten way to pay him back for helping, even if it was unintentional. If what he said was true and Danny hadn't been able to get back, she would have spent a very miserable night out in that storm. Now there was the warmth of a fire and a roof overhead, such as it was. With a shudder Coley glanced around the dismal room.

She slipped off her wet sandals and placed them by the hearth to dry. The zipper of her flowered dress refused to budge and only after she had contorted her long arms into several ungainly positions was she able to unzip it and fight herself out of the clinging wet garment. Carefully she placed it on the back of a chair near the fire. Now that the car was gone it was all the clothing she had. The remnants of her shredded hose she peeled off rather sadly, using the more substantial portions to wipe the mud from her slender legs before tossing the ruined nylons into the fire. Shivering with the cold, Coley gathered the blanket around her and moved closer to the fire's heat. Little rivulets of water trickled from the curling strands of her hair on to her angular face where she impatiently brushed them away.

A crash of lightning accompanied the opening of the door as the tall stranger stomped in. He removed

17

his hat with an impatient movement of his hand before shaking free of the slicker. Timidly, Coley watched him hang them on a hook inside the door. His hair was black and straight, the sides and back were long and plastered against his neck by the rain. In a stifling silence he walked to the hearth, unbuttoned the top of his shirt before pulling it over his head. The naked expanse hypnotized Coley as she stared at the bronze back tapering from wide shoulders to a narrow waist. When he turned his chest with its cloud of dark hair towards her, she gulped and clutched the blanket a little tighter. But his eyes flicked over her to the chair where her forlorn flowered dress lay. Immediately two circles of blue fire leaped back to her.

'I told you to take your clothes off, and I meant all of them!'

Coley managed a stiff, negative shake of her head while her body attempted to shrink inside the blanket. Her eyes widened in fear as he took a step towards her. Her gaze was riveted to the scar on his face, its white jagged line resembling a lightning bolt across several days' growth of dark stubble. He stopped. His mouth was drawn into a grim line and his teeth clenched tightly, flexing the muscles in his lower jaw.

'I've seen female undergarments before, if that's what's worrying you,' he murmured, his voice soft and almost gentle, but the diamond-like quality in his eyes revealed the hidden hardness of his tone. His upper lip curled slightly as he added, 'And if it's the other thing that's worrying you, I prefer my women more amply endowed. I leave children alone.'

He didn't seem to expect a reply from Coley as he walked to the far side of the room, taking the lantern with him. She watched him hang it on a hook near a makeshift cupboard.

'I'll see if I can find us something to eat while you finish undressing,' he said, and turned his head to look at her. 'You are hungry?'

Coley nodded hesitantly up and down, never taking her eyes off the stranger. He continued to stare at her across the room before remarking very quietly, 'I won't watch.'

With that he turned back to the cupboards and began opening doors. Coley studied his back for a moment before standing. She glanced around her for a moment seeking some place to change, out of sight if possible. Finally she manoeuvred the chair her dress was on over to the bed. There she used the blanket to make a screen behind which she could undress. The sounds of water being pumped from a hydrant assured her that her companion was occupied and that she was in comparative privacy. With as little wasted motion as possible she pulled the slip over her head, letting it drop to the floor while she worked at the hooks on her bra. Finished, she searched for an inconspicuous place to dry them before putting them on the open chair with a sigh. Shivering now from her nakedness and the cold, she hurriedly wrapped the blanket around her.

'There's some hot tea here whenever you're ready,' the man offered.

Coley shuffled across the room, aware that two spots of red were staining her cheeks.

'I'll have some, thank you,' she stated, coming to a halt a few feet from the stove.

He looked down over his shoulder at her bare feet before raising his gaze to her button nose and hazel

19

eyes. His eyes were like a mirror, showing nothing of their owner's emotions, but reflecting the looker's attempt to hide her embarrassment.

'I'm nineteen,' Coley declared, sensing a need to defend her status of womanhood.

'Really?' he nodded before turning to pour the strong, black tea into a metal cup. 'The food will be ready shortly.'

'Can I help with anything?' Coley asked, stung by his off-hand manner at her previous statement. When an eyebrow raised over a blue eye, she added, 'I can cook.'

'With that blanket as a handicap, you'd be more of a hindrance than a help.' The sharp tone dismissed her offer.

Slightly hurt by the unqualified rejection even though the reason was accurate, Coley shuffled over to the table and sat in one of the chairs where she sipped her tea in silence. A few minutes later a brown hand placed a plate heaped with beans, fried Spam and whole tomatoes before her. Coley issued a polite thank you without looking at her companion before picking up her fork to eat.

'It's not exactly gourmet food, but it's hot,' was the reply as the man sat down in the chair to her left.

It was a struggle eating with one hand holding the blanket around her while the other attempted to get the food to her mouth without the blanket slipping. It was a slow process that her rescuer seemed ignorant of, his attention never leaving his plate. Finally, covering a white shoulder for the fifteenth time, Coley pushed the plate away, her hunger abated and her discomfort growing.

He glanced up at the scrape of the plate. 'More

tea?'

Coley shook her head negatively. She watched silently as he cleaned his plate and rose to pour some tea for himself.

'Is there a ranch house near here that my brother could have reached?' Coley asked, watching the muscles of his bare arm as he stirred sugar in his cup.

'The Simpson place is about three miles from the crossing. I'm sure he made it to there.' His glance at her was inquisitive with a slight hint of arrogance about it. 'Just where were you going?'

'To stay with our aunt,' Coley answered, adding in a smaller voice, as she lowered her gaze to a crack in the wooden table, 'Danny said she doesn't live very far from here—on a ranch.'

'What's the name of the ranch or your aunt? I might know her.' He sat his metal cup on the table and turned his compelling eyes to her.

Nervous under the demanding gaze, Coley stammered, 'Her-her n-name is Wilhelmina Gr-Granger and she lives at the Slash S.' Tension filled the air as the stranger's eyes narrowed at her words. 'Is that far from here?'

'She is expecting you?' he asked as if he knew the reply would be negative.

'She invited us,' Coley skirted his question as best she could without lying. 'Do you know her?'

'Yes.' He pushed his chair from the table and stood up. 'You must be getting cold. Go over by the fire and I'll wash up.'

'Does she live nearby?' Coley persisted, not wanting the conversation to end now that she had found someone who knew her aunt.

'Yes. You're on the Slash S ranch now.'

21

'You work for her.' A degree of relief was in her voice.

'No, her brother-in-law, Ben, owns the ranch. You might say I work for him.' His words emerged slowly and concisely through tightly compressed lips. His calculating gaze seemed to be daring her to ask any more.

Coley sat quietly huddling in her chair while she solemnly watched him as he gathered the dishes. She started to shiver again, but whether it was from the cold or the oppressive atmosphere that had suddenly engulfed her, she couldn't tell. Silently she rose from her chair and shuffled morosely to the fireplace on the other side of the room. She stared into the flickering flames trying to shake the feeling that she and Danny had jumped from one unpleasant situation into another. Had it been the reticence of the stranger or the bitterness and suppressed anger in his voice that had made her feel this way? Or was it her imagination running away with her because of the thunderstorm outside and the vicious scar on his cheek? If only Danny were here!

A movement behind her roused Coley out of her contemplation. She turned to see her companion remove the mattress from the bed. She studied his rough-hewn features, wondering again at the apprehension that was growing inside of her at the prospect of meeting her aunt.

'It will be warmer for you sleeping in front of the fire tonight,' the man said, placing the flimsy mattress behind her.

'Where will you sleep?' Coley asked, submissively lowering herself to her makeshift bed to sit cross-legged on it.

'In a chair,' he replied, poking the fire and adding another log to it. 'I've slept in more uncomfortable places.'

'Do you know my aunt very well?' Coley blurted out, the tension building inside her at her unknown destination and its occupants. 'We've never met her before and I was wondering what she was like.'

'Sometimes it's wise to find out for yourself. Other people's opinions are not always right,' he answered cryptically.

'But——' Coley began.

'I suppose I should at least know the name of the girl I'm spending the night with,' he commented, but without a teasing smile on his face.

Coley blushed furiously.

'Colleen McGuire, but Danny calls me Coley,' she replied. Gathering courage, she continued, 'I'm sorry about the way I looked when I saw your scar. You see,' she hurried as his taciturn expression stiffened, 'I was already frightened by the thunder and lightning when you found me. And you seemed so angry that I was a little scared of you, too. I guess seeing the scar just took me by surprise.' His face had become a mask, with blank blue eyes. 'It really doesn't look that bad, sort of like a dueller's scar, a badge of courage,' Coley suggested, trying desperately to undo the damage she was doing by bringing the subject up. But the cynical smile that appeared confirmed her failure. Hanging her head, she stared down at her hands. 'I'm sorry. I shouldn't have said anything.'

'It's all right, Coley.' He hesitated over her name. 'Your comparison is quite different from the Biblical one that I usually hear.'

'The mark of Cain,' Coley whispered hoarsely,

wishing she could take back the words the minute she had uttered them.

He stared at her quietly before rising from his chair to extinguish the lantern. In the semi-darkness the flames from the fireplace danced eerily on his face, accenting his brooding look.

'You mean your brother...' Coley began, the chill of his words creeping up her back.

'We'd better get some sleep. We've done too much talking already.' His voice was bland and unrevealing.

Confused and uneasy, Coley stretched out on the mattress, cradling her head on one arm as she stared into the fire. Raising her head, she looked up at the man in the chair, his head resting against the back and his eyes closed. Sensing her gaze, he opened his eyes and looked down at her.

'What's the matter?' he asked, not changing his position.

'I don't know your name,' Coley answered, an apprehensive but subdued expression on her face.

'Jason.' He added with the barest ghost of a smile, 'My friends call me, Jase. Good night, Coley.'

'Good night, Jase.'

CHAPTER TWO

THE horse lifted his feet high as he picked his way down the slope. Coley swayed with the gentle rocking motion, her slender body in unison with the man in the saddle. The horse's coat, that had glistened so blackly in last night's rain, now gleamed blood-red in the morning sunlight. On the road below them was a car with two figures watching their approach. Coley recognized one as her brother and presumed that the other was the rancher whose help Danny had sought.

Although Coley was relieved at the sight of her brother, she couldn't summon much gladness. The apprehension she had felt last night had not eased with the morning light. Her scarred companion Jason had been even less communicative this morning than he had last night, nodding only a hello when he had entered the cabin to find her dressed and drinking the tea he had left for her. He had informed her that the horse was saddled and he was ready to take her to her brother. And that had been the sum total of the conversation for the last fifteen minutes.

There had been so many questions Coley had wanted to ask him, about her aunt, the ranch and everything. But the tight lips and calloused features very clearly closed the door on any conversation. Very soon now she would be finding all the answers herself, but the chill shuddering through her told her she wasn't going to like them.

It was a very serious-faced Danny who helped Coley down from the horse. His anxious eyes examined her stained dress and uncombed hair for any tell-tale signs of trouble that he should know about.

'Are you all right, Coley?' When she nodded affirmatively, he added, 'Are you sure?'

'I'm fine,' she assured him.

'I tried to get back last night, but the water was too high. I nearly went crazy thinking about you out there in the storm all night. I should have taken you with me somehow,' he remonstrated himself.

'I was all right. There's a cabin on the other side of the rise and I—we spent the night there,' Coley replied, her face reddening slightly with her words. She glanced self-consciously over to where Jase stood talking with the other man.

'Mr. Simpson told me about it, but I couldn't help thinking that you might not find it,' Danny answered following her gaze to the man she had ridden in with. His eyes narrowed on to her face. 'He treated you all right, didn't he?'

'Yes, I was frightened at first, that's all,' she replied, avoiding Danny's searching eyes for fear they would find the pinpricks of doubt that were troubling her. 'He works at the ranch for Aunt Wilhelmina's brother-in-law. She doesn't own the ranch, Danny!'

'I know.' His words carried a grim tone that did little to boost Coley's confidence. 'I got our clothes and all out of the car. It got swept downstream by the water last night.'

'Will it still run?'

'Not till I can get it pulled out and check it. Even then...' His voice trailed off expressively. He looked at his sister's face, reading the anxiety written there. If

Aunt Wilhelmina couldn't or wouldn't take them in, they had no money and now no transportation to take them away. 'Don't worry, Coley, everything will be all right, I promise you.'

'But, Danny, what if . . .'

'If you two youngsters are ready to go, we'll leave now,' the man who had been talking with Jase interrupted.

'Of course, Mr. Simpson,' Danny answered, leading Coley to the car where the two men were standing.

Two hard blue eyes studied her brother thoroughly as Danny made the introduction of his sister to the rancher. But other than the sharpness of the gaze, the expression was bland when Danny turned to Jase. Danny's eyes too were drawn to the scar shining out from the beard growth before being drawn to the piercing eyes, but this time there was no reaction from Jase, the mask securely on his face.

'I want to thank you, sir, for taking care of my sister,' Danny said, extending his hand.

Jase accepted it and merely nodded his acknowledgement, before gathering the reins and mounting his horse. His face was now hidden in the shadows of his hat brim as he lifted his hand in an indifferent good-bye and trotted his horse away from the group. Coley stared after him.

'Ahh,' Simpson sounded as though he was trying to rid his mouth of a bad taste. 'He's a cold one.' Danny glanced at the rancher suspiciously, seeking an explanation for the remark, but receiving only, 'Come on. Let's go.'

Silently, brother and sister slid into the front seat with him. The closing of the door seemed to echo the closing of the last door of escape for the two. From here on they were committed to whatever lay ahead.

The morning sun peered through the dotted swiss curtains at the curled, sleeping figure half out and half under the chenille bedspread. Outside birds were trilling to the morning breeze, their muffled calls reaching the tousled figure of Coley as her eyelids lifted slowly from their heavy burden of sleep. She blinked bewilderedly at her unfamiliar surroundings. Then yesterday's memory drifted back. She pulled herself into a sitting position, then bent her legs so that her slender arms could hug her knees. All the despair from yesterday came echoing back as her sad eyes gazed forlornly at the rose-flowered wallpaper.

All her misgivings had loomed larger during that silent ride to the Slash S ranch house. Had it been Danny's moodiness or the skeleton-faced Simpson's ominous silence that first made Coley aware that some of her fears might come true? She knew that Danny had found out something that had shaken his confidence when all her arguments had failed. If only that stranger would have told her more!

When they had come to a stop in front of the large two-storey wood-frame house, gleaming whitely through the leaves of the large oak trees, Coley's heart involuntarily leaped with joy at the serene picture. But that was before Mr. Simpson spoke.

'Sorry, boy,' he had said, 'looks like the old man is sittin' on the porch. Much as I hate to, I'd better go up with you.'

Coley had started to ask Danny what Mr. Simpson was talking about, but he had already opened the door and stepped out of the car. Barely able to stem the rising panic, Coley followed him, brushing vainly at the stained spots on her dress and trying to force the wayward strands of her brown hair into some semblance of order.

Coley leaned forward and chewed on a fingernail without relaxing her hold around her legs as she remembered meeting the man that Simpson had referred to as the 'old man'. The wheelchair he was sitting in had drawn her attention first, but when Mr. Simpson had introduced him as Ben Savage, Coley had looked at the man. He was an eagle; age had made him a grey eagle, but an eagle all the same. His keen grey-blue eyes had inspected them thoroughly from beneath the bushy eyebrows. His head was covered with an abundance of white hair streaked with grey. Only the sallow colour of his skin and the way it hung so loosely on his face and neck betrayed the state of his health.

Mr. Simpson had explained to him that Danny and Coley were Wilhelmina's nephew and niece and had come for a visit. He had told him about their car and implied that both had spent the night at his ranch. Coley had been too awed by her prospective host to correct Mr. Simpson. Ben Savage had watched them carefully while the rancher was talking, taking in the mud stains on Coley's dress and their general appearance of something less than prosperity. He had said not one word of greeting to them. His words echoed back in their hopelessness to Coley.

'I had hoped I'd seen the last of sponging relatives,' he had said, smiling slightly maliciously when Danny bristled. 'But since I haven't, she's out back in her rose garden.' The directness of his gaze had silenced any remark from Danny. 'I'll be talking to you two tomorrow.' Then he had turned his wheelchair and left them with his unvoiced threat hanging over them like Damocles' sword.

A silvery white head peeped around Coley's bedroom door.

'Are you awake now, dear? You looked so exhausted last night that I said to myself, "Now you let that dear child sleep as late as she wants in the morning." '

'Oh, Aunt Willy, is it very late?' Coley asked with a note of alarm as she hopped out of bed. 'I don't want Uncle Ben to think that I sleep late all the time.'

Coley and Danny had been given very positive instructions by Aunt Willy that even though there was no blood relation they were to refer to Mr. Savage as Uncle Ben. Coley couldn't think of anyone less like an uncle.

'Oh, fiddle what Ben thinks,' Wilhelmina stated as she set a stack of clothes down on Coley's dresser. Coley marvelled again at the tall woman's erect posture. 'Maggie washed up some of your clothes.' She opened and closed drawers with little wasted motion. 'Colleen, I'm terribly sorry to tell you this, dear, but that terrible river water just about ruined everything. Just look at this skirt—or worse, this blouse!' With a horrified expression she held up a faded navy skirt and a very worn white blouse before placing them in drawers. 'We'll just have to go on a shopping expedition,' she went on cheerfully. 'I haven't been on one in ages.'

Coley walked over to the mirror, picked up a brush and began pulling it through her hair. She was too embarrassed to correct her aunt about the state of her clothes. Wilhelmina Granger walked over to stand behind Coley, her taller frame enabling her to see over Coley's head into the mirror. She took the brush from Coley, her bracelets jingling, and began expertly brushing here and fluffing there.

'Your hair needs a good styling, too,' she remarked to Coley's red-faced reflection in the mirror. 'Now, don't you go getting all upset about it. If your dear mother, Rosalie, were here you know she would have seen that your hair was properly cut.'

Coley nodded silently, hanging her head so that her aunt couldn't see the moistening eyes. How could she tell her that she'd never had her hair done by a professional?

'Colleen, listen to me, dear,' Wilhelmina Granger turned the girl towards her and lifted her chin gently with the tip of a red-varnished fingernail. Coley looked up at the generous red mouth, the rouged cheeks, the bright, jewelled glasses that winged over her aunt's blue eyes. 'I know sometimes I'm a silly old lady who's a little absent-minded at times. The Good Lord didn't see fit to give George and me any children, but now he's given me you and Daniel. Forgive me if I get too interfering or sentimental, because, you see, you mean very much to me.'

'Oh, Aunt Willy!' Coley smiled gratefully through her tears.

'Well.' Aunt Wilhelmina inelegantly sniffed back her tears. 'We'd better stop this or we'll both be crying. You'd better hurry up and get dressed. Maggie's got breakfast ready downstairs. Hurry up, now.'

She smiled as she pushed Coley towards the bed before walking out the door in tune with the jangling of her bracelets. Coley clasped her arms about her excitedly. It was a glorious feeling to be wanted, abso-

31

lutely glorious! Hurriedly she slipped off her night clothes and began dressing.

Coley trailed her hand down the banister of the open staircase. Her eyes roved contentedly through the hallway below her as she slowly made her way down the steps. Her sandalled foot was on the last step when one of the doors in the hall opened and a slender, dark-haired man emerged.

'And you tell Jase I want a full accounting of his absence,' came the gravelly voice of Ben Savage from inside the room. 'It's about time he learned that nobody disappears from this ranch for three days without me knowing about it and knowing where they are and what they're doing.'

'Yes, sir,' the man replied with a deferential nod of his head before closing the door. But his expression when he turned towards Coley was anything but respectful.

Coley noted the thin face, the sleek black hair, the black, snapping eyes, the fine winged brows and the thin lips with their almost insolent curl. When he saw Coley, his mouth immediately changed its expression to a charming smile, although she saw his eyes narrow before becoming a part of the widening smile.

'Well, good morning. You must be Colleen.' He extended his arm, an even golden brown colour from the rolled-up short sleeve down to his long fingers. 'Aunt Willy told me all about you.'

Coley shyly accepted his hand, slightly intimidated by his effervescent air. 'How do you do.'

'I can tell she forgot to tell you about me. That's just like her,' he grinned to show a flashy expanse of white teeth. 'I'm Tony Gordon, the old man's nephew.'

Coley glanced apprehensively at the closed door.

'He's rather in good form today.' Tony grimaced playfully as he followed her glance. 'Where were you going, the dining room?'

She nodded.

'I'll escort you there. I won't be able to stay, though I imagine Aunt Willy will be there. I've got to go find Jase and then I'm supposed to meet your brother and show him around,' he stated cheerfully, taking her elbow and guiding her down the hallway.

'Has my brother talked with Mr. Savage this morning?'

'He was going out as I was coming in.'

'I hope Danny didn't say anything to upset him,' she murmured.

'Knowing Uncle Ben, I doubt if he got the chance,' Tony laughed. He turned his young face with its merry glint in his dark eyes towards her. 'I suppose your turn is coming yet.'

'I'm supposed to go in to talk to him this morning,' Coley replied. Some of her earlier good spirits deserted her as they reached the sun-filled dining room,

'And the condemned ate a hearty breakfast,' Tony teased, pulling out a chair for Coley at the table.

'Tony, stop that,' reprimanded the silver-haired woman already seated.

'I was only joking, Auntie dear.' But his joke had stolen Coley's appetite.

'You pay no attention to him, Colleen.' Aunt Wilhelmina began passing dishes to Coley with her nervous, busy hands. 'You run along, Anthony. Daniel is waiting for you outside.'

Tony waved a cheerful good-bye to Coley, who

could barely manage a smile in return. She nibbled half-heartedly at her toast and pushed her scrambled eggs around on the yellow flowered china plate while her aunt chattered in her blithe, ebullient way.

'Colleen dear, you've hardly eaten a thing.' Her aunt's red lips were pursed poutily. 'We'll never cover those bones sticking out through that blouse.'

'I'm sorry, but I'm just not very hungry,' Coley replied apologetically. 'I've always been skinny anyway. I never have been able to gain weight.'

'You'll be grateful for that one day.' The older woman sipped her coffee with her little finger raising unconsciously. 'And you mustn't be upset by your slenderness. I'm sure you realize that there are many fashion models who would love to have your natural figure.'

'But they have faces to go with them,' Coley said, forcing a lightness into her voice to hide the inner hurt.

'You aren't unattractive, Colleen,' Aunt Willy stated briskly. 'A little plain, perhaps, but that can be changed. Now, if you really are done with your breakfast, Benjamin wanted to see you privately in his study.' Aunt Wilhelmina rose from the table, smoothing her skirt with her hands. The rings on her fingers flashed brilliantly in the sunshine. 'And don't you let Anthony's teasing upset you.'

'No, Aunt Willy.' Coley stood resolutely.

If only she could forget Tony's teasing. If only she didn't feel as if she was going to an inquisition with herself as the victim. Her long legs moved her slowly down the hall to the study. Why did she have to be so afraid of everybody and everything? Danny had always been there to get her out of tough spots, but this

34

time he wasn't there and she was on her own. She just couldn't go into that room knowing how that old man in the wheelchair would mock her. That was it. He was in a wheelchair; he was a sick man like her mother had been. Many times during the years that Coley had nursed her mother, the distress had become more than her mother could bear and she had been irritable and snappy. Uncle Ben must have the same problem. And her mother hadn't liked Coley to change things, clinging steadfastly to the familiar. That would explain why Uncle Ben resented her and Danny being there, disrupting his household. She had never been frightened of her mother, so why should she be frightened of Ben?

A bright light now gleamed in her eyes as she rapped lightly on the study door.

'Come in, come in,' was the gruff reply.

Coley stepped into the oppressive study. The maroon drapes were closed, shutting out the morning light while the dark panelled walls added to the gloom. She glanced at the grey-haired man behind the desk. He didn't look very sick.

'Would you like me to turn on a light?' Coley asked timidly.

'What's the matter? Can't you see?' he growled.

'It is a little dark in here.'

'It's foolish to have the electricity on during the day. A waste of money! The sun's plenty of light,' his tone reproached her sharply.

Coley glanced over at the closed curtains, wondering if she should say anything more. 'Perhaps I could open the curtains?' she suggested hesitantly.

'Persistent little snip, aren't you?' Coley swallowed nervously waiting for him to speak again, not trusting her voice not to tremble. 'Think it'll improve my sunny disposition, do you?' His eyes squinted threateningly at her, a glint of humour lurking at the corners. 'Very well, open them, if it pleases you.'

Gratefully Coley walked over to the window and pulled the cord to the maroon curtains, allowing the sunlight to tumble in.

'Satisfied?' he snorted. He waved a bony hand towards the chair in front of his desk. 'Come over here and sit down, now that I can see you.'

Coley did as she was directed and managed to sit quietly under his disconcerting stare. She rather liked his sarcastic humour. It made him a little more human and gave her a little more courage.

'There's not much to you,' he said disparagingly. 'Can't you do anything with that hair of yours? It looks like you forgot to brush it.'

His blue-grey eyes saw her look at his own bushy hair. 'I don't like backtalk, so you might remember that,' he said severely. 'Now, let's get down to business. There's no such thing as a freeloader on this ranch. Everybody pulls his weight or leaves.' He paused to allow his words to sink in. 'What are you good for?'

'I can cook and clean,' Coley answered, 'and I took typing in school, but I'm not very good.'

'We got a housekeeper and the house isn't big enough for two. Don't need any typing done. What else?'

'I nursed my mother for several years.'

'I don't need any nursemaid!' he bellowed, raising himself in the wheelchair.

'No, I didn't mean ... I mean...' Coley stammered. She leaned forward, her smooth forehead

36

drawn together in an anxious frown.

'Get out of here! Go on!' Ben shouted, running a gnarled hand through his grizzled hair.

'I'm sorry.' Coley's round eyes began to mist with tears. 'I just don't know how to do many things.'

'I'll find something for you to do,' he growled. 'Now, get out of here. I've heard enough of your prattle. Your aunt will be wanting you anyway.'

Coley rose numbly from the chair. Through the shimmer of tears, she saw Ben's hand plucking nervously at the chair handle. She ruined everything. She should have known how sensitive the poor old man would be about his incapacity. Why couldn't she have been more tactful? Twice now since coming here, she had referred to two people's afflictions, first Jason's and now Uncle Ben's. When would she learn to keep her big mouth shut?

When she reached the study door, Coley turned back towards her uncle seeking the words to undo the damage. The forlorn picture of the invalid staring blankly out of the sun-filled window hushed her words, and she silently closed the door behind her.

An hour later she wandered out into the shaded backyard where her aunt was busily at work among her roses. Coley watched indifferently the sure clipping of the scissors in the gloved hands. The floppy straw hat picturesquely framed the silver-white hair while protecting the face from the steady rays of the sun. Coley approached her aunt slowly, trying to phrase the words that would explain her unsuccessful meeting with Uncle Ben.

'Colleen dear, I wondered where you were,' her aunt's voice sang out. 'I was dusting my roses. Don't you just love roses? They have such a classical but intricate design to them that they never cease to delight me. The buds are so fragile and delicate, and the full blooms are so rich and velvety. But the fragrance is like a heady wine, sweet and tantalizing.' Fervidly she turned, expecting Coley's affirmation. But Coley hadn't been following her aunt's words. She was wrapped up in her worries about Ben Savage. 'What's the matter, dear? Didn't your talk with Benjamin go well?'

Coley shook her head glumly.

'Let's go over here and sit down,' Aunt Wilhelmina said, pulling off a glove and placing the varnished-nailed hand on Coley's shoulder. She guided her towards a group of lawn furniture under a spreading oak. 'You can tell me all about it.'

Slowly Coley began her story, stuttering for the words, then rushing incoherently when she couldn't find them. She ended in a burst of tears.

'There, there,' comforted her aunt. 'I probably should have mentioned to you how touchy he is about his paralysis. He didn't mean anything by it. I'm sure he was sorry for his temper afterwards. He likes to think of himself as so independent of anyone else that the least reference to the fact that there's something he can't do for himself sends him into a rage. He knows you aren't the kind of person to mean anything by it.'

'I hope so, Aunt Willy,' sobbed Coley, twisting her hands nervously in her lap. She looked earnestly in her aunt's face. 'I tried to tell him I was sorry.'

'It's best not to say anything. Pretend that everything went well and forget that burst of temper of his.'

'But it happened!'

'Of course, but bringing it up won't make you or Benjamin feel any better about it, now will it?'

38

reasoned Aunt Willy.

'No,' Coley agreed, wiping the tears from her cheeks and smiling into the jewelled eyeglasses.

'I have an idea. Benjamin always likes some tea before dinner. Why don't you go to the kitchen and have Maggie fix a pot? Then you can take it to him as a sort of peace-offering.'

'All right.'

'Put a cold cloth on those eyes of yours first,' instructed Aunt Willy, rising as Coley did. 'Otherwise he'll recognize those red eyes and swollen lids as the result of a good bout of tears and will feel twice as guilty.'

'Yes, Aunt Willy,' Coley called back, already hurrying back towards the white house.

Entering the back door into the kitchen, she spied the housekeeper cleaning some vegetables over the sink. Quickly she walked over to stand beside the thin, middle-aged woman.

'Aunt Willy suggested I see if you could fix a pot of tea for Uncle Ben.'

'I've already got it brewin' on the stove and the tray is sittin' on the table,' the woman answered tersely, the rhythmic strokes of the brush unbroken by the conversation. 'T''will be ready in a jiffy.'

'I'll take it in to him as soon as I clean up,' Coley replied, a little awed by the businesslike housekeeper.

The cold of the washcloth felt good against her face. After a few applications, the redness left and the swelling was down. Coley's cheeks looked quite pale, so she pinched them tightly to bring the blood to the surface. She really felt much better. Quickly she hung the towel and washcloth on the rack and hurried back to the kitchen. The flowered teapot was now sitting on the tray with the cup and saucer.

'If you'd like me to come back and help you, I will,' she offered as she picked up the tray.

'I've been doin' everything by myself for eight years, I guess I can do it for eight more,' Maggie retorted, her back to Coley.

Feeling she had already put her foot in her mouth once today, Coley left without saying anything else. She hummed happily as she walked down the hallway towards her uncle's study. At least she could let Ben know that she held no hard feelings towards him. A few steps from the open door she heard someone talking.

'We only lost four head to the flood.' It was Jase with Ben.

'You could have sent out one of the hands to find that out,' Ben said irritably.

'I needed the air.'

Coley stopped short of the doorway, sensing a hostility in the conversation.

'Oh, you did, did you! Here I thought maybe you'd left for good.' There was a trace of sarcasm in the invalid's words.

'You should have learned by now I'll never leave,' Jase's voice raised to emphasize the last word. 'As long as there's an inch of land left that's Savage land, I'll be here. You might as well get used to that fact.'

Curiosity drove Coley to the doorway to view the tall, broad-shouldered man leaning on the desk towards the old man in the wheelchair. The bitterness and hatred etched on their faces stunned her.

'You should have left! No murderer will ever get one grain of dirt on this ranch!' Ben cried.

'Then you'd better throw me off.' Coley watched

horrified as anger twisted Ben's face at Jase's words. 'But you can't, can you! And furthermore, you wouldn't if you could,' Jase went on sarcastically. 'Because you need me. Your precious Tony would destroy everything you've worked for in a week. You need me!'

In a fit of frustration, Ben wheeled his chair away from Jase to stop with his eyes on Coley. At Ben's startled expression, Jase turned, too. It took but an instant for him to assess the horrified and incredulous expression on her face before he turned away towards the window.

'I brought your tea, Uncle Ben.' Coley's small voice was followed by a heavy silence.

'Bring it in, girl,' he instructed gruffly.

She practically ran into the room, the tea cup rattling in its saucer in protest. All the while her mind raced. Was Jase going to speak to her? Would he tell Uncle Ben they'd spent the night together during the storm? What would she say if Uncle Ben introduced them? But Ben had no such intention.

'Thank you,' he said as she set the tray down on his desk. 'You can go now.'

She nodded and turned towards Jase. He still hadn't shaved, though now the beard almost covered the scar, but nothing covered the ice-blue eyes that challenged her. She hesitated only momentarily in front of him, drawn to him in spite of her fear, just as she had been that night, before she rushed out of the room.

CHAPTER THREE

COLEY stared out her bedroom window nibbling unconsciously the nail on her forefinger. She had come upstairs to dress for dinner. Aunt Willy told her it had been the custom for many years to dress for the evening meal. It was exceedingly easy, Aunt Willy said, to sit down in workclothes, bolt your food and finish the evening in a state of apathy, but dressing up made you feel like a new person; a leisurely meal gives an atmosphere of congeniality; and the evening takes on a refreshing air. It all sounded very grand to Coley if she could just shake off the uneasy feeling she had.

On the surface everything was just the way she had always dreamed a home would be. The house was roomy and comfortable. Aunt Willy was sweet and caring. Even Ben was likeable in spite of his gruffness. But underneath was a foreboding of the hidden things she didn't know; things that could destroy her precarious sense of security. And Jase was the key to it all, the man who had rescued her in the storm, who, even though he frightened her a little, had made her feel safe and protected.

She stared down at the bold flowers splashed on the synthetic material of her dress. The mud stains were all gone now, thanks to Maggie. It was her best dress, but Coley knew it didn't measure up to Aunt Willy's sophisticated tastes. It was just a cheap dress different from her others only because she bought it and it

42

wasn't someone's hand-me-down. She glanced out the window again. Her morose expression lifted as she recognized her brother walking through the yard gate. She rushed quickly out of the room and down the stairs to be at the door when her brother entered.

'Danny!' she cried gaily. 'I've been watching for you to come.'

'Hi!' He wrapped an arm around her shoulders and continued towards the stairs. 'What have you been doing all day?'

'What have *you* been doing all day?' Coley countered. 'You were gone before I got up and I missed you for lunch.'

'Can't you tell what I've been doing?' he smiled. 'Smell.'

'Whew!' she exclaimed, inhaling deeply next to his shoulder.

'I had the glamorous job of cleaning the barns.' He grimaced playfully at her before scooting her on ahead of him up the last step.

'Oh, poor Danny,' Coley laughed. She swung his hand happily as they walked down the hall to his bedroom. 'Thank heaven, we're supposed to dress for dinner or Aunt Willy would never allow you at the table. Did you know about that—dressing for dinner, I mean?'

'Yeah, Tony told me about it.' He unbuttoned his shirt to take it off. 'Now tell me, what have you been doing.'

'Nothing.'

'Nothing? Did you go in and talk to the old man?' His brown eyes watched her reaction carefully.

'Yes, I did,' Coley answered, seating herself on his bed. But her thoughts weren't on her meeting with

43

him, but on the conversation she had overheard between Ben and Jase.

'How did it go?'

'All right, except he doesn't know what to do with me.'

She plucked nervously at the chenille bedspread.

'Don't worry about it. I told him I'd take care of paying for your keep.' He rolled his shirt into a ball and tossed it in the hamper. He smiled over at her. 'Of course, he assured me that I would.'

Coley smiled in understanding. 'What did you think of him, Danny?'

He paused before answering. 'I like him. I mean, he's rough and says what he thinks, but I like him.'

'So do I.'

'When I was out there cleaning the barn, I thought about how he can't even get out there to see if I'm doing my job. He's got to be hard or everything he's worked for will crumble away. Do you know what I mean, Coley?' She nodded. 'I don't feel sorry for him. You can't pity a man like that even if he is an invalid. I said as much to Tony, but he just laughed. I don't think he understood what I meant.'

Jase's words rushed back to Coley. 'Your precious Tony would destroy everything you've worked for in a week.' She sat silently on the bed, debating whether she should tell Danny the things she had overheard.

'Come on,' her brother said, taking hold of her hand and pulling her off the bed. 'You'd better clear out. I've got to shower and change yet and your jabbering is holding me up. I'll meet you downstairs.'

'Okay.' She left the room meekly, not yet willing to put her thoughts into words.

'Colleen! Oh, there you are,' said her aunt, standing at the bottom of the stairs. 'Would you help Maggie set the table? I haven't got the flowers done yet or I'd give her a hand. I didn't realize it was so close to dinner time.'

'I don't mind,' Coley answered, skipping on down the steps.

'Is your brother ready yet?' At Coley's negative shake, Aunt Willy pursed her lips nervously. 'Well, it never takes men long to get ready,' she mused, and bustled Coley into the dining room. 'The silverware is in the china cabinet over there. The rest of the things Maggie has in the kitchen.'

Coley glanced around at the six plates resting on the white tablecloth. 'Is Maggie eating with us tonight?'

'Oh, no, dear. She says that hopping up and down is bad for her digestion, so she eats later.'

'Who's the extra plate for?' Coley asked.

'Oh, didn't I tell you? Benjamin's grandson will be here for dinner this evening. Now really you must hurry. The men will be coming in shortly and the table won't be ready.'

Coley placed the silver around the table, filled the glasses with iced water, and brought in the necessary salt, pepper, butter, sugar and cream containers from the kitchen. Danny entered the room as Aunt Wilhelmina was putting the finishing touches on the centrepiece and Coley was ticking off on her fingers the various items on the table.

'Is dinner ready?' Danny asked, stretching and patting his stomach hungrily.

'Mmm,' Aunt Willy answered absently, stepping back to admire her handiwork. 'We'll be sitting down presently. My, but you look nice, Daniel.'

Coley glowed at the praise for her brother. His

crisply starched white shirt and brown trousers did make him look rather attractive, especially with his fresh scrubbed face, and the water still clinging brightly to his immaculately combed hair. A murmur of voices sounded from the hallway.

'That will be the men coming.' Aunt Willy adjusted the strand of pearls around her neck and patted the silver waves that wouldn't think of being out of place.

Coley and Danny turned to the arched doorway expectantly. Ben wheeled in first, his grizzled hair still bushily denying any efforts from the brush.

'I certainly hope dinner is ready by now, Willy,' he grunted.

'Of course it is, Benjamin. We always eat at this time,' Aunt Willy admonished, accompanying her brother-in-law to his place at the head of the table.

Tony followed his uncle into the room, smiling at Danny and slapping him on the back.

'How are you feeling? The old muscles tightening up yet?'

'Some,' Danny smiled, his head cocking inquiringly at the man now standing in the doorway. He glanced at Tony and added, 'I guess I'm not used to it yet.'

'You will be,' Tony nodded with a mock grimace. Turning towards the doorway, he said, 'I don't think you've met our new guests, Jase.'

Coley stood transfixed staring at the man in the doorway. His beard was gone, revealing the strong cheekbones and sharp jawline. The scar wasn't as visible against the tan of his cheeks as it had been. His straight black hair was still too long and his icy blue eyes hadn't lost their brilliance. He looked younger, in his early thirties. His clothes were different. In place of levis were trimly tailored blue slacks topped with a

46

lighter blue shirt. He looked so distinguished, so commanding and slightly ruthless. He was walking forward. Coley dimly heard Aunt Willy making the introductions, catching the words only half-consciously.

'—my sister's daughter's children. Colleen, Daniel, this is your Uncle Ben's grandson, Jason Savage.'

Jase held out his hand to Danny. 'I understand you had an unfortunate experience with our floods,' he said.

Danny cocked his head bewilderedly, then with dawning comprehension, he took Jason's hand and replied, 'We're lucky we were able to get to the Simpson ranch.'

Jason turned to Coley. 'I'm happy to meet you.'

Coley awkwardly placed her hand in his warm, firm handshake. She couldn't speak. She just swallowed and nodded.

'Did you want me to start servin' dinner now, Mr. Savage?' Maggie asked from the kitchen doorway.

'Of course,' Ben scowled. 'I'm not sitting here for want of a better place. Providing that you're finished with all of your polite amenities, Willy.'

'I believe we're ready to sit down, Maggie,' Aunt Wilhelmina agreed with a stately nod. 'I hope you will remember, Benjamin, about quarrelling at the table. It's very bad for the digestion.'

Jase had pulled out the chair on his grandfather's left for Coley before walking around the table to sit at Wilhelmina's left. Coley glanced hesitantly at her brother beside her, but he frowned at her slightly to signal silence. She clinched her hands tightly in her lap, watching the dishes pass from Uncle Ben to Tony on to Jase and Aunt Willy. She tried to act as nonchalant as everyone else, to assume the indifferent mask that Jase wore, but it was impossible for her. She jumped every time Ben grumbled a sentence, expecting each time that the arguing would start, and a little more tense each time that it didn't.

'What did you do today, Coley?' Tony asked, flashing his white teeth at her from across the table.

'I helped Aunt Willy in the garden,' stammered Coley, almost dropping her fork as she spoke. She felt her cheeks flush as Jase glanced at her.

'What did dear Uncle Ben decide for you to do around here?' Tony grinned, eyeing his uncle mischievously.

Coley averted her eyes to her plate and waited breathlessly for him to answer. Not for anything was she going to let Tony know how rotten her interview had turned out.

'She's worthless for anything but ornamentation,' replied Ben, scowling at her through his bristly brows. 'The way she looks right now she ain't much good for that either. Willy, you're going to have to get something done about her hair. It's always sticking out all over.'

'Like yours, Uncle?' Tony teased.

'Don't be insolent!' Ben glared at his nephew. Looking back at his sister-in-law, he continued, waving a fork in the air as he did so. 'Get her some decent clothes, too. Next time she comes to dinner I want her dressed for it and not looking like a ragamuffin.'

Shame and humiliation welled up inside Coley. She blinked desperately, aware of Jason's stare. Coley glanced quickly at her brother. The back of his neck was turning red, but his mouth had clamped shut on his anger. For Danny, this was their last chance and they must make a home here at any cost, even their pride.

'Really, Benjamin, must you be so blunt?' Willy scolded. 'You are so utterly tactless at times. I had already planned to take Colleen shopping tomorrow. Most of her clothes were damaged in the flood, so of course, her clothes would be in a disgraceful condition.'

'I'm sure Colleen will enjoy the shopping trip,' Jase said, sending a small smile of assurance in Coley's direction.

'Of course she will. All we girls do.' Aunt Willy stretched her red mouth into a playful, conspiratorial smile.

'Yes, it will be fun.' Coley's words trembled only a little, but she knew it was enough to betray her.

'Nonsense!' snorted Ben. 'You females just like to spend money.' He reached over and laid a gnarled hand on Coley's arm. 'But you be sure to pick out something nice for dinner tomorrow. I'll expect to see a pretty little lady sitting next to me.'

His words touched Coley as she sensed that he was, in his own way, apologizing for his bluntness. She felt Danny relax a little, too.

'Maggie!' Ben bellowed. When she finally poked her head around the door, he said, 'We'll be having our coffee on the porch.' As the chairs scraped the polished wood floor, Ben turned to Coley. 'Well, are you going to help me or not?'

She nodded slightly and stepped behind the wheelchair to lead the entourage out to the porch. As she manoeuvred the chair through the screen door and on to the porch, Coley heard the lowered voice of her aunt speaking.

'You are coming out with us for a little while, aren't you, Jason?'

'No.' His voice was clipped and hard.

'But, Jason——' her aunt began plaintively.

Coley glanced at the other three on the porch. Danny and Tony were talking and Ben was staring out into the sunset. Only Coley's ears were straining to hear the conversation inside.

'I will not be a party to any of your conciliatory attempts. It's no use,' Jase said sharply. 'Leave Ben and me alone. There's nothing you can say or do that can change the past. Leave us with our mutual dislike.'

Coley's eyes mirrored the confusion and pain that was on Willy's face as she stepped through the light bathing through the screen door on to the porch. Her aunt glanced beseechingly at Ben, but he was staring unseeingly at the crimson glow above the hills. Coley tensely watched the flustered woman who had become embedded in her heart in the last thirty-six hours. She saw her shoulders straighten and the sagging chin lift, before her aunt seated herself next to Ben, regaining her grace and dignity. Coley remained in the shadows apart from the group. Her heart contracted in pain while she watched the flashing red nails of her aunt's hands as she poured the coffee. When the same hands were done with their task and one went to its owner's throat to click the beads together nervously, Coley knew she could watch no more the agony that was burning inside her aunt and slipped unnoticed off the porch into the yard.

Silently, not wanting to be seen or stopped, Coley followed the evening path of shadows to the back of the house. At last out of sight, she slowed her steps

50

and began wandering aimlessly among the stately oaks. Her thoughts became jumbled and incoherent. Flashes of her night spent with Jase came searing back, but mixed up with the never-ceasing echo of Ben's ringing 'Murderer,' 'Murderer,' 'Murderer!' She glanced bewilderedly up to the evening sky with its smattering of stars, only to see once again ominous rolling clouds splintered by forks of lightning before they were blocked out by the vision of a jagged white scar against a black beard and her own taunting words, 'Mark of Cain.' Her lids closed tightly over her hazel eyes trying to shut out the pictures she was seeing. What had happened that could cause such hatred between grandfather and grandson? Why hadn't Jase told her that night that he was the grandson of the owner? Why had he let her think he only worked on the ranch? He must have known she would find out.

Danny had had such high hopes for them. Her generous mouth turned up slightly with affection for her brother. He had wanted a family and a home for her. She had both and now wanted desperately to belong, but this family was torn apart by hate and mistrust. A sickening feeling knotted itself in the pit of her stomach at the thought of continued arguments such as she had heard today between Jase and Uncle Ben. Coley, who hated any disagreement, who couldn't cope with bitter words from people she cared about, shuddered in fear. Jase couldn't be a murderer, she told herself. If he really was, he would be in prison. Somewhere there were answers, a solution. That was what she must find.

Suddenly, amid the shrilling cries of the cicadas and crickets, Coley heard the rasp of a match being struck behind her. Her spine tingled in apprehension as she turned towards the sound and murmured hoarsely:

'Who's there?'

Without answering, a figure stepped out of the shadows, shaking out the match as he did so. The light of the quarter moon illuminated the blue shirt and then the face of the figure. Jase walked slowly towards her, the gentle glow of a lit cigar in his hand.

'Good evening again, Miss McGuire,' he murmured very politely. 'It's a lovely night for strolling through Aunt Willy's rose garden, isn't it?'

Her body tensed as he stopped beside her, barely controlling a wild desire to flee. His blue eyes challenged her, but only briefly as she turned her head away from his face. Did he know or had he guessed that she had overheard him talking to Aunt Willy? Did he think she had expected to find him out here?

'I needed some fresh air and I was too restless to sit on the porch with the others,' Coley explained breathlessly. She glanced up at him hesitantly and had the peculiar feeling that those piercing eyes saw right through her.

'We all are in need of fresh air after dinner,' he replied grimly. 'Did you enjoy the evening meal?'

Coley knew he wasn't referring to the food and lowered her head to stare at the ground rather than reply.

'You'll probably have difficulty adjusting to the peculiar structure of our family, but I'm sure in no time you'll be like the rest of us,' he mocked.

'Are you really Ben's grandson?'

'Yes.' His smile as he answered was cynical with a bitter twist to the corners of his mouth. 'You find that hard to believe, don't you?'

She nodded silently. A large, calloused hand gripped her elbow and they began walking as if he could bear no more to stand in one place.

'You overheard a great deal today in Ben's study, didn't you?'

'Yes,' Coley answered, acutely conscious of the burning restlessness of the man beside her.

'That was unfortunate,' he stated, taking a puff from the cigar before hurling it into the night.

'I don't really understand,' Coley said, glancing hesitantly at his masked face. 'Why do you ... dislike each other so? What happened?'

His short laugh was embittered with anger. 'That's a long story that has been told too many times. It's better that you don't know. You're incapable of taking sides and you would be torn apart like Aunt Willy is. Let it be.'

'How?' Coley asked. Her eyes grew rounder in her effort to understand. For a moment she thought she saw a reflection of the pain that she felt there in the recesses of his glance. But he turned away.

'You're not a murderer!' Her protest was vehement, though spoken softly.

'I'm not?' It was a question and not a statement, but it held a bitterly sad note that drew an involuntary sob of pain from Coley.

'I see your dress is none the worse for the storm,' he observed, his hand still guiding them as they walked aimlessly among the roses.

'No,' Coley replied quietly. She was grateful for the change of subject and yet wishing Jase would talk about the other. 'It still is a pretty awful dress.'

'No, no, it isn't.' Jason's voice was almost gentle with a bit of the reassurance that he had attempted to give her at the dinner table tonight. 'But I'm sure

53

you'll find a lot more that you will like better when you're shopping tomorrow.'

From the near side of the house came shouts of laughter and splashes of water followed by more boyish cries. She glanced questioningly at him.

'Tony and your brother must be swimming. Would you like to go and see?'

She nodded agreement and they turned towards the house. The bright lights at the pool blinked saucily at them through the thick branches of the oaks, lighting their way to the pool and sundeck surrounding it. Coley and Jase stood on the extreme outer edge of the sundeck out of reach of the exuberant sheets of water that sprayed from the hands of the two swimmers. Coley watched the wet gleaming bodies of her brother and Tony enviously as they gambolled in the water like two playful seals. She felt Jason's eyes on her and smiled up at him briefly before turning back to the pool.

'Hey, Coley!' Danny cried, waving an arm at her. 'I wondered where you were.'

'Go and change,' Tony ordered, his dark hair glistening blackly in the lights. His white teeth flashed brightly. 'Come on in. The water's fine.'

'I can't,' Coley called back, a shy smile lighting her face. 'I haven't got a swimsuit.'

'Who cares?' hooted Tony, pulling himself on to the sundeck amidst another flood of water. He laughed merrily at her blushing cheeks. 'Willy can fix you up with something. Come on in.'

'No, thanks,' Coley smiled. The envy crept into her eyes as Tony jack-knifed into the water near Danny.

'Do you know how?' Jase asked astutely.

'No,' Coley's voice was soft and shy. 'I've never

learned.'

'Would you like to?'

'Of course,' she replied. Her eyes beamed up at him with the hint of a dream peeping through. 'It always looks so graceful.'

'If you'd like, I'll teach you,' Jase offered, staring out into the pool at the shimmering lights on the water.

'Would you really?' Coley exclaimed excitedly. 'I mean if it's not too much trouble.'

'I wouldn't have offered otherwise.' He gazed into her happy face. 'Be sure to have Aunt Willy buy you a suit when you go shopping tomorrow.'

'Oh, I will,' Coley cried delightedly. 'When can we start?'

'Day after tomorrow,' he answered. 'I always take a morning swim at six, if you can get up that early.'

She glanced up at him, expecting to see a teasing glint in his eyes, but his expression was just as undefinable as it always was. 'I'll be there,' she promised solemnly, as if she were taking an oath.

'Fine. Good night, Coley,' Jase said with a polite nod to her.

'Good night, Jase,' Coley answered as he walked from her towards the house. She watched his tall figure for a moment, hugging her delight to her, before she turned back to the two swimmers in the pool. Soon she would be like them. Very soon.

Coley chewed nervously on her fingernail as the two women studied her reflection in the mirror of the beauty salon. She felt small and insignificant as her aunt plucked at a strand of Coley's hair and discussed it with the heavy-set stylist, Gloria. The hair stylist nodded an agreement with something that Aunt Willy had said and then stepped behind Coley's chair to skin the hair back from her face, turning and tilting her head this way and that, like a mannequin. A comb appeared from nowhere and began fluffing here and there.

'Okay, little lady,' she said to Coley, swinging the chair away from the mirror, 'let's get down to business.'

Somehow Coley managed a weak smile of agreement before she was whisked out of the chair and placed in the hands of a shampooer who was given explicit instructions for the type of shampoo, rinse and conditioner. It seemed to Coley that she had barely relaxed under the brisk, vigorous fingertips of the shampooer when a towel was wrapped around her head and she was bustled back to the stylist. Her hair was combed out and sectioned, before the hum of scissors began snipping away. Out of the corner of her eye, she watched strands of hair falling to the floor with a precision-like rhythm. Then deft flicks of the wrist began inserting rollers in her hair until Coley stared into the mirror at her head full of rollers. She submitted numbly to the strong hand of the stylist as she was led to a row of dryers where she was inserted under one of the hoods and left.

Her head felt strangely heavy and cumbersome. Never had she ever been in a hair salon. Any cutting or trimming that had to be done in the past had been done by one of their neighbours who had once studied to be a beauty operator. But now here she was, in a salon filled with immaculately dressed women walking in and out, their hair gorgeous and sophisticated. She couldn't suppress a little thrill that maybe she would look a little bit like that. The steady rush of hot air that had flushed her cheeks stopped and Gloria was beside her bustling her off to another chair, this time with an array of cosmetics spread out before it.

Again Aunt Wilhelmina was beside the stylist, only this time her silver hair was in rollers too, outlining the heavily made-up face like a comical hat. Gloria was holding Coley's arm while she tested various bases with her skin. Brisk instructions were given to Coley while the selected base was applied to her face, but Coley was too excited to really listen as she should. Next came the eye-shadow, a rich shade of olive green that brought out the green flecks in her hazel eyes, then the mascara which darkened her lashes and further enhanced her eyes and finally a pale peach-tinted lipstick was applied. Then she was off, back to the chair where she had started, and the rollers were being taken from her hair. Coley gasped with pleasure as she saw her formerly limp, wayward mouse-brown hair bounce and curl about her face with a golden-brown sheen to it.

'Now I've used a colour rinse to bring out the blonde highlights in her hair,' Gloria was saying to Willy. 'It really won't be necessary once she's out in the sun, because it will bleach out on its own.'

All the time the stylist was talking, a brush was vigorously going through Coley's hair. It was replaced by a comb and the styling began. With miraculous flips of the wrist, feathers of hair curled here and there, changing from wayward wisps to flattering waves. Her reflection no longer showed a thin, angular face, but a delicate and attractive face with an awed expression transparently obvious in the rounded eyes.

'Aunt Willy, is that really me?' Coley exclaimed, half fearfully.

'Yes, dear,' her aunt answered, her red lips smiling

widely. 'Gloria, it's perfect, absolutely perfect. You are a remarkable woman!'

'So are you, Mrs. Granger,' the stylist replied, basking unashamedly in the praise. Gloria whisked away the plastic cape from around Coley's shoulders and applied a healthy amount of hair spray to hold her creation in place. 'You, little lady, are very beautiful. You deserve to be proud.'

'Thank you, thank you so much,' Coley answered breathlessly, not wanting to take her eyes off her reflection in the mirror.

How long it took for Aunt Willy to be combed out, Coley had no way of knowing. She was too enchanted with the new 'her' to care. To Coley, in no time at all they were walking out the door of the salon and Aunt Willy was chattering about which shops they were going to and what types of clothes Coley was going to be needing. And Coley was swept into another breathless whirl. It didn't matter what she tried on, pant suits, everyday shirtwaist dresses, party dresses, short sets, jeans—she looked gorgeous in everything. Once when she heard Aunt Willy tell the sales lady they wanted three more pairs of jeans and to show them some knit tops, Coley couldn't help feeling a twinge of guilt at the cost of all this.

'Aunt Willy, this is going to cost too much money,' she whispered.

'Don't you be worrying about such things, Colleen,' admonished her aunt. 'You need the clothes and I'm enjoying every minute of it.'

Coley was too. Never had she ever dreamed she could look as pretty as her reflection kept telling her she was. Each time she looked in the mirror she would reverently put a hand to touch her hair, the feathery, wavy strands that looked so carelessly wind-blown and free. But when she tried on the yellow whipped-cream dress with little cap sleeves and eyelet lace around the yoke and a pair of matching yellow low heels, she stood in front of the dressing mirror in a trance. She was beautiful, really and truly beautiful.

'Yellow is your colour!' Aunt Willy exclaimed. Her bracelets jingled loudly as she clapped her hands together in appreciation. 'Miss,' she called to the sales lady, 'bring me that chiffon party dress, the yellow one on the mannequin.'

'That will look very charming on her,' the woman replied.

'Aunt Willy, I don't really need another dress. This one is perfect,' Coley finally managed to speak.

'Nonsense. That's a perfectly good dress, but you're going to need a party dress. You should have several of them, but we don't have a very big selection to choose from here. One or two will have to do for now.' With her usual efficiency, Willy took charge of fitting the chiffon dress on Coley.

Aunt Willy was right. Coley looked and felt like a fairy princess in the dress. It floated in soft buttercup folds around her, softening the thinness of her body into an ethereal ray of sunshine, all golden and airy.

'We'll need some accessories with that,' her aunt murmured. 'We'll go and pick those out as soon as you change, Colleen. With this dress, I think we've got everything you're going to need for a while. Change into that slack set, dear.'

'Aunt Willy,' Coley called hesitantly as her aunt started to turn away.

'Yes, dear?'

'I—I don't have a swimsuit,' she stammered.

'Oh, good gracious! I completely forgot about it,' Aunt Willy exclaimed. 'Of course you must have one. I guess I didn't think about you swimming.'

'I—I don't know how yet,' Coley answered, flushing in embarrassment.

'You don't? Who is going to teach you? Daniel?'

'No,' Coley replied, hesitating a little over her next words, unsure of how her aunt would react. 'Jase said he would teach me. If that's all right with you.'

'Of course it's all right,' Aunt Willy replied. But her blue eyes were narrowed by the frown on her forehead. 'Jason is going to teach you?'

'Yes, Aunt Willy,' Coley replied.

'That's strange,' said Aunt Willy, more making a comment to herself than talking to Coley. 'We'll have the sales girl find something for us in a swimsuit.'

That evening Coley rapped lightly on her brother's door. She was wearing the yellow dress with the eyelet lace around the yoke. She had been staring at her reflection for the last hour. Even though she realized how vain she was acting she was enchanted with herself. When she had heard Danny leave the shower and return to his room, she had raced across the hall so that he would be the first one to see the new Coley.

'Danny, it's me! Open up,' she whispered.

As the door swung open by her bare-chested brother, the towel still vigorously drying his hair, she twirled happily into the room.

'Coley!' Danny's voice was as dumbstruck as she had expected it to be. 'Is that really you?'

'I'm beautiful, Danny!' Her words ended in a merry laugh as she danced around his room. 'You should see all the wonderful clothes Aunt Willy bought me. My hair ... don't you love it!'

'My sister, Cinderella!' Danny laughed, the pride glowing like a neon light on his face. 'May I have the privilege of escorting Your Highness to dinner this evening?'

He bowed low before her, his towel flung in front of him like a cape. She laughed merrily and curtsied.

'I would be delighted, sir.'

'Then you'd better scram out of here so I can get dressed,' he said, turning his towel into a whip.

She laughed again and danced out of the room. A few minutes later he was at her door, offering her his arm down the stairs. Coley felt like a princess making her grand entrance down a winding staircase. The new pride and assurance gave a previously hidden dignity and grace to her slender body. When Danny opened the door to the dining room for her, she walked unhesitatingly into the room, totally conscious of the pleasing picture she made. Her hazel eyes gleamed brightly at the group already seated at the table. Tony rose immediately from his chair, the stunned surprise showing on his face. Her gaze softened as she looked at the agreeable smile on Ben's face as he looked at her.

'Aunt Willy,' Tony exclaimed, walking around the table to stand in front of Coley, 'you're a fairy godmother!'

Coley's eyes turned to Jase, expecting to hear an echo of Tony's words or at least, the unspoken praise that was in Ben's eyes, but the mask was there, if anything, more firmly in place than ever. Her expression flickered briefly in hurt and confusion before taking Tony's arm with a gay smile. If she had looked at her aunt, Coley would have seen an equally puzzled face studying Jase very intensely.

The meal was just a continuation of a dream for Coley, a dream that had long been dreamed. Tony fairly danced attendance on her, flattering her with his words and eyes. Even the gnarled man in the wheelchair went out of his way to be chivalrous towards her. And the few times she glanced into her brother's eyes, the glow of pride was there for everyone to see. Except for Jason's silence, everything was complete. When they finally all withdrew to the veranda, Coley was pleased and surprised to see Jase join them. She took a seat on the bright wicker settee, feeling deliciously like a coquette with Danny on one side of her and Tony on the other and Jase smoking one of his slender cigars in the chair next to them.

Coley tilted her head towards Tony, confidence dazzling her smile. His slender brown arm rested lightly behind her shoulders while his dark eyes snapped messages to her.

'Were you really surprised over how I changed?' Coley asked, knowingly seeking a compliment, but too full of her own satisfaction not to want it voiced by another.

'You knocked me cold when you walked into that room, Coley,' he affirmed, his gaze roving over her face while drinking in her loveliness. 'It was like seeing the cinder girl turn into Cinderella complete with Aunt Willy as fairy godmother. And me playing Prince Charming, stunned into adoring speechlessness.'

Coley's laugh lilted over the porch, intoxicated by his compliments. This for her was all her Christmases gathered into one day.

'I felt like a princess today,' Coley said softly, almost in fear of breaking the spell of enchantment that surrounded her. She gazed unconsciously at Jase as she spoke. 'Just as if the clock would strike any moment and I would be chanted back into that sad little urchin that always looked back at me from the mirror. Do I look different to you, Jase?'

He, of all people, must see the change from the drowned little girl he had rescued to this innocently sophisticated young woman. Her eyes gleamed brightly in the dim light as she waited in anticipation for his answer. And he must agree, the change was too apparent.

'You don't look like a princess at all to me,' he replied. His voice was brittle and in the dim light, Coley was hurt to see the extension of his nostrils in controlled anger. 'Tony is quite mistaken.'

Coley gasped uncontrollably at the censure in his voice. His eyes sought her out.

'You remind me of one of Aunt Willy's roses,' he said. His gaze softened ever so slightly, although his expression never changed. 'One of her yellow rosebuds, filled with the purity of innocence and just beginning to open into a full bloom.'

His soft yet distinct words echoed into a deepening silence on the porch. Coley's eyes misted brightly at the praise, so unqualified and so full of a promise to her as she matured.

'So words still come easily to your lips, huh?' The gravelly voice of Benjamin Savage sliced like a rapier into the silence.

Jase failed to answer the sarcastic question as he snubbed his cigar out in the ashtray on the table beside him.

'If you'll excuse me,' he murmured, rising and nodding towards his aunt as he spoke.

Coley watched as he descended the veranda steps into the night. His walk was slow and his posture erect. Coley turned to her uncle to protest, but was silenced by a sharp nudge from Danny.

CHAPTER FOUR

COLEY watched the long, gleaming form slicing effortlessly through the water, shimmering a pale blue in the morning sun. She was late, she knew, for her lesson, but the graceful, rhythmic strokes of the brown arms fascinated her with their precision. Would she ever get over her own fears and be able to swim like that? Coley wondered.

This morning would mark her fifth lesson and she still shivered apprehensively at entering the pool. Only the deep desire to learn drove her on, making her overcome the quaking of her body. It wasn't so bad now as it had been that first morning when Jase had had to practically help her into the water. Coley had been surprised at his patience with her. He had taken her step by step, until she understood. He took the fundamentals slowly, persuading her to immerse her head in the water and blow bubbles, letting her hold on to the side of the pool as she kicked her feet with a scissor-like movement and instructing her in the arm movements that he was now doing so effortlessly.

He reached the opposite end of the pool and stopped, shaking the water from his black hair with a twist of his head. Holding on to the edge of the pool with one hand, he waved a greeting to her with his free hand.

'Oversleep?' he asked as Coley walked shyly to the edge of the pool.

She nodded sheepishly before shrugging off her terry-cloth robe to reveal the two-piece swimsuit with its bright yellow flowers. Coley hurried into the shallow end, just a little embarrassed by her scanty attire. Jase swam slowly down to her end of the pool, stopping a few feet from her and letting his feet settle to the bottom as his chest and head raised out of the water. His hands carelessly swept the water from his face and the hair from his forehead before coming to rest on his hips.

'We'll practise some more floating today,' he said, his blue eyes abstractedly taking in her appearance. He moved away from her in the water and instructed, 'Float over to me on your stomach and remember to keep your head in the water.'

Taking a deep breath, Coley allowed herself to slide into the water, her arms outstretched and reaching for the solid, reassuring hands of her teacher. Within a few seconds of time, that seemed like minutes, she felt two hands catching hold of hers and lifting her upwards. She wiped the water from her face and looked to him for approval. As usual, there was nothing but the mask.

'Okay, let's do it again.'

Twice more she floated slowly towards him and twice more after that with the accompaniment of the scissor-like motion of her legs.

'All right,' said Jase, looking expectantly at Coley, 'we're going to learn the backfloat now. It's easy. Just relax like you did before and I'll hold you up.'

Obediently Coley turned her back to him and supported herself on his arms. But as the water swirled around her face and over her head, she sputtered to the surface and gripped his arm in panic.

66

'It's all right. Come on, lean back now,' his patient voice instructed. Again she leaned into his arms, unconsciously stiffening her body as she did so. 'Relax. Don't tighten up.'

Shutting her eyes to close out her inner fear, Coley surrendered herself to the firm hands supporting her shoulders and her back until the buoyancy of the water claimed and soothed her. It wasn't so hard, she thought to herself, as the little waves lapped around her body. It was fun! She felt so serene and at peace floating like this in the water. Unknowingly, a happy smile had curled her generous mouth.

'You're enjoying it, aren't you?' Jase asked, his complacent tone answering his own question.

'It's so peaceful,' Coley breathed, her voice tinged with the mystification that she felt. She opened her eyes to look up at him, seeing with pleasure that his own eyes were almost smiling back at her.

'You're not afraid any more,' Jase replied as Coley closed her eyes again. 'Move your hands a little bit to propel you through the water.' When she began to move her arms away from her sides and sink, he quickly repeated himself, holding her up in the water with his hands. 'Just your hands. Just move them a little bit.'

This time she just moved her hands back and forth and thrilled as she felt her body being pushed along by her own movement. She sighed dreamily, relaxing now in the comfortable motion of the water.

'I really am going to learn how to swim, aren't I, Jase?' she asked, opening her eyes to look into his face.

But it wasn't there! Suddenly she missed the pressure of his hands on her back. In terror she turned her head swiftly to see him treading water just a few feet away from her. And then everything went wrong. Her long legs tumbled over themselves in a desperate effort to find the bottom that wasn't there. Her arms began flailing the water as she panicked from the water swirling around her head.

'Jase!' she gurgled, striking out desperately towards him. She saw him moving towards her as she tried to make her arms move in the synchronized rhythm that he had shown her. Then she was in his arms, being pulled towards the edge of the pool, coughing and spluttering as she went. When they had reached safety, her arms remained clasped around his shoulders, her body trembling and shivering with fright.

'You're all right, now,' Jase said, his arm remaining firmly around her bare waist. 'You did fine. You actually swam to me.'

'I ... I did?' she stuttered, her terrified eyes gazing into his as she huddled closer to him, grateful for the broad, tanned chest to lean on. 'Why di-did you let go of me?'

'Because you didn't need me. You were floating all by yourself and I was in the way,' he answered patiently, smiling comfortingly into her face.

'I really did?' Coley asked, warming to his praise, in spite of her previous scare.

'Yes, you did.' His smile was so gentle and unexpected that she could only stare at his lips, growing slowly more conscious of the few inches that separated them and the suddenly burning touch of his hand on her bare midriff. His head began to bend towards hers as her eyes remained hypnotized by his mouth.

'What have we here? An early morning rendezvous?' came a teasing voice from the pool side.

Almost roughly Jase pushed Coley away from him, yet not letting her go, as they both turned towards the mocking face of Tony.

'I was just giving Coley a swimming lesson,' Jase retorted sharply at Tony's raised eyebrows. 'She had a scare in the deep water.'

'And Daddy was going to kiss her little fears away,' Tony finished in mock-adult baby talk. Colour rose high in Coley's cheeks as she left the protection of Jason's arm and edged her way along the side of the pool to the shallow end. The scar on his cheek stood out whitely as Jase glowered at Tony before moving after the retreating Coley.

'If that's the way these little swimming lessons are turning out,' Tony said, 'I'd like to stand in for you one of these days, cousin dear.'

He grinned widely at the pair before striding off jauntily towards the ranch-yard, whistling merrily as he went. Coley watched him leave, wondering how she could look Jason in the face after what almost happened. She knew he was standing just a few feet from her in the shallow water, his piercing blue eyes watching her.

'Had enough for today?' His voice rang harshly in her ears as she nodded her assent.

He was waiting by the ladder, one arm gripping the rung and the other resting impatiently on his waist. She longed to run past him, but the water tugging at her legs reduced her pace to an ungainly waddle. Coley kept her head lowered, hiding as best she could the red flush on her cheeks and the misting of her eyes as she groped blindly for the ladder. As his hand gripped her arm to steady her when she stumbled on one of the rungs, she almost ripped it away from him in her shame. Somehow she made it to one of the lounge chairs and began towelling herself off with the little dignity she could muster. She silently wished he would grab his towel and leave as he usually did. This time he hovered above her like a hawk over his kill. She tried to ignore him. She had to, she couldn't face him, not in the state she was in.

His hand reached out and imprisoned her chin, twisting her face upward to his. She could feel him studying her intently, but Coley couldn't look into his face. Just as suddenly as he had grabbed her, he let her go, walking a few paces to her right where his towel lay. Involuntarily her ears followed his movements, hearing the crackle of paper and the striking of a match. Her nose smelled the aroma of the little cigars he always smoked. Again she felt his eyes on her.

'I told you you were too sensitive,' Jase said briskly. 'If you're going to last around here, your skin's going to have to toughen.'

Then he was gone. She clutched the towel tightly around her shoulders, hugging it close to her. He was right, she was too sensitive. What a silly thing to get so upset about! It was Tony's fault for teasing them, that was what had embarrassed her so, not the thought that Jase might have been going to kiss her. Heavens, she didn't even know if that was what he was going to do. Suddenly Coley realized that she had wanted him to. Momentarily stunned by her discovery, she stared blankly into the pool.

She had always shied away from any close contact with the opposite sex, especially after that repulsive episode with Carl. But a few minutes ago when Jase had held her, it had seemed almost instinctive. In that one brief moment when his head had begun to bend towards hers, Coley had actually felt that it was natural and right. Was that where her shame came from, from her own bold desire and not from Tony's teasing, but from his catching her in that vulnerable moment?

Visibly subdued, she made her way into the house and up the stairs into her room, her mind conscious of only this confusing revelation.

She spent the rest of the morning trailing after her aunt as Willy made her daily rounds in her rose garden. If she noticed Coley's inattention to her conversation, she made no mention of it. The whole family was present for lunch, a rare occurrence since quite often one or several were out on another section of the ranch. Somehow Coley managed a small smile when she looked at Jase, her round eyes expressing the apology for her morning conduct that she was too shy to put into words. With a barely perceptible nod, Jase accepted it.

Danny's expression was a little grim when he sat down beside her while Tony winked at her from across the table. Coley fought for a calm composure although she was aware that there were two bright dots of colour on her cheeks.

'How are your swimming lessons?' Tony asked with a malicious twinkle in his eye. Danny stabbed at a pea on his plate.

'Very well,' Coley replied, accepting a dish from Ben with just the slightest tremor. 'I'll soon be as good as you and Danny.'

'As soon as you get to the advanced level, why don't you let me take over for Jase?' Tony gleamed at her, flashing his white teeth at her in a knowing smile. 'I'm an excellent teacher.'

His barely disguised innuendo flooded her cheeks as she concentrated her attention on her plate. She glanced briefly at Jase, meeting the full force of the piercing gaze. He was waiting for her reply too. She mustn't let Tony's teasing get to her. She had to show Jase that her skin was tough and she could take it.

'Really, Tony?' she replied as coolly as she could. 'I never would have guessed that you were experienced in the teaching class.'

Tony's head jerked back at her words as he glanced over at Jase, but not quick enough to see the sly smile that Coley saw before it was quickly suppressed by a studied concentration of the steak he was slicing. She could have almost giggled with her delight, but she turned instead to her brother, anxious for a change of subject.

'What have you been doing this morning?' she asked.

'Taking care of a mare that just foaled,' Danny answered, a hard glint in his eye as he looked at his sister. 'It's a late foal and we've been keepin' a close eye on it.'

Danny couldn't keep the pride from sneaking into his voice.

'A little baby?' Coley exclaimed, captured by the excitement of birth. Turning excitedly to Ben, she asked, 'Can I go down and see it?'

'Of course. Danny can take you down after lunch,' Ben smiled good-humouredly.

'Will you, Danny?' Her eyes gleamed.

'Sure. But you'll have to change into some jeans. Those shorts aren't exactly the thing for a barn,' Danny stated.

'Right away,' Coley cried happily, pushing her chair away from the table. 'May I be excused, please?'

'You haven't had your dessert yet, Colleen,' admonished Aunt Willy.

'I'm not hungry. I'll have it later,' Coley called, already at the doorway. She started to leave the room, then ducked her head back in. 'You be sure and wait for me, Danny.'

'I will.' His voice sounded disgruntled, but there was a happy expression on his face as she returned his smile and bounced out of the room.

Coley raced up the steps into her room, creating a small whirlwind when she got there as she rummaged through her drawers for her jeans and a top. She changed in record time, then stopped in front of the mirror to touch up her hair briefly with a comb and add a hint of the peach lipstick. She wrinkled her button nose at her reflection and dashed out of the room. She arrived breathless at the bottom of the stairs and hurried to her brother, who was waiting only slightly impatiently at the door. With a cheery 'I'm ready' from Coley they left the house.

Coley managed to slow her anxious feet to the sedate pace her brother was taking. She flashed a happy smile at his sombre expression, taking his arm with a childlike gesture.

'What are you so serious about?' she asked, hugging his arm while giving him a saucy smile.

'What happened at the pool this morning?' His question was so unexpected that Coley couldn't suppress a little gasp. She had no trouble now slowing her previously bouncy steps to his.

'You talked to Tony, I suppose,' Coley replied, astutely recognizing the tale-carrying culprit.

'He said he saw you and Jason in a little clinch.' His words came out slowly through gritted teeth, but there was concern and speculation in his eyes when he glanced at his sister.

'That's not the way it was,' Coley replied, going on to explain about her fright in the deep end of the pool and Jason's rescue. 'I was just hanging on to him because I was frightened. And that's when Tony came along.'

'So that's all there was to it,' Danny breathed. The relief etched little curves around his mouth.

'Well——' Coley drawled, desperately seeking the words that would explain her confused feelings. She had always confided in her brother and she needed to again. He was always able to put things in their right order. 'Not exactly. You see, Danny,' she rushed, 'afterwards I got this feeling that I would have liked him to kiss me. I don't really understand it. That's why I got so embarrassed at Tony's teasing, because I wanted it to happen.' She paused briefly. 'I've never felt like that, especially after Carl...' Her words drifted away into silence.

'Coley, there are some things you don't know about Jase.' Danny spoke hesitantly.

'I overheard Jase and Uncle Ben arguing one day shortly after we came here.' Coley spoke very low so that Danny had to bend his head to hear. 'Uncle Ben called him a murderer. That's what you're talking about, isn't it?'

Danny studied her very intently before answering.

'Yes, that's what I'm talking about. I've heard things, stories, I don't know how much of them are true, but either way, he's thirteen years older than you. He's ... I don't know, only I don't want you getting too close to him or you're going to get hurt.'

That was the second time she'd been warned off, the first time by Jase himself, Coley thought as they reached the stables. Did she seem so much like a child to everybody that they couldn't trust her to judge the facts?

As they walked down the roofed breezeway and past the stalls, Coley looked around her. She had been so engrossed in her conversation with her brother that she hadn't noticed her surroundings. This was the first time she had ventured into the actual ranch-yard and she studied the various buildings and corrals with interest. Several hundred yards away she noticed a large barn surrounded by heavy reinforced fencing. She could barely make out the distant grey shapes within the fences.

'What's over there?' She directed Danny's attention to the distant corrals.

'In those enclosures? Brahma cattle,' he answered. 'They raise them for rodeo stock. I understand Jase had been doing some experimental breeding with them, too. They're a hearty breed, able to stand up under the hot weather and insects better than the Herefords and Angus. They're awful touchy, though, so don't you go hanging around those corrals. They didn't build those fences like that for nothing.'

Coley gave a little shudder, remembering pictures she had seen of rodeo bulls tossing riders and clowns around. No, she wouldn't be going near them.

'Here's the little mother,' Danny crooned, stopping beside the open foaling pen at the south end of the stable. He reached out and laid a reassuring hand on the shiny brown neck of the mare. He took hold of his shy sister and drew her up beside him to see the

75

spindly-legged colt sprawled exhaustedly on the hay. 'Here's the Johnny-come-lately.'

As if the mare knew that Danny was showing off her son, she turned her head and nickered to the sleeping colt. He raised his too large head in answer and then attempted to get his long legs in the correct position to get him on his feet. After several awkward attempts that brought quiet gasps of laughter from Coley, he made it and stood staring at them, brightly swishing his furry whisk-broom of a tail arrogantly.

'He's all head, ears and legs,' Coley laughed, delighted with the comic little colt.

'He'll grow into all three,' Danny promised, scratching the mare's forelock as she nuzzled him for her share of attention.

Coley tried coaxing the little man over to her, but he just shook his blazed face at her and dashed, as best he could, to the protection of his mother's flank.

'Coley, do you like it here?' Danny asked unexpectedly, turning an anxious face to her. 'I mean, do you want to stay? I don't really get to be with you very much and if you're unhappy ...'

'Oh, no, I like it here,' she inserted quickly. 'Aunt Willy is so good to me that I feel guilty about not being able to pay my way. But, Danny, I wish you wouldn't work so hard. You're always off in the barns or stables somewhere.'

'You know something, I like it. It's all so interesting that it doesn't seem like work,' Danny replied earnestly. 'Can you imagine that, a city boy like me? But there's so much you have to know to be able to operate a ranch successfully, especially one of this size. Do you want to see some of the other horses?' he asked as if suddenly self-conscious of his enthusiasm.

'Yes,' Coley replied, following Danny as he walked away from the pen.

When they reached an adjacent corral, Coley climbed on to the top of the fence beside Danny, barely concealing her dismay as the horses within trotted over to them.

'They won't hurt you,' Danny said as a bold sorrel horse bunted his arm playfully. 'They just want some attention.'

Hesitantly Coley placed a careful hand on the head of a small bay and made a haphazard job of scratching his head as she had seen Danny do. As another horse moved in making Coley feel like she was being surrounded, she scooted closer to Danny. The new horse, a blaze-faced chestnut, nuzzled her arm.

'His nose is so soft,' Coley exclaimed, turning her hand palm upwards as the horse investigated it. 'It feels like velvet.'

She gradually grew more confident, not jumping every time one made a move that she wasn't prepared for, until she was laughing along with Danny at the spats of jealousy that took place between the horses. They were so engrossed in the little byplays that they failed to hear Jase ride up behind them.

'Why don't you take your sister out for a ride?' he said to Danny, almost startling Coley off her perch.

Danny looked at his sister before issuing a rueful snort that said 'forget it' very plainly.

'I'd love too,' Coley murmured wistfully, 'but ...'

'I know, you don't know how to ride.' Jase laughed, a warm delicious laugh that tingled through Coley. 'Do you want to learn?'

'Sure, but ...' said Coley, slipping down off the fence, followed by her brother.

'Danny could teach you,' Jase suggested.

'Oh, no, not me,' Danny cried, begging off with grim determination. 'I've been through that before. Her decisions last about as long as it takes to saddle a horse and then she's gone.'

'Do you want to learn?' Jase repeated, the two blue diamond eyes challenging her.

'Of course,' Coley asserted, indignant and a little put out by her brother's evaluation of her weak determination.

'Grady!' Jase called, turning in his saddle to hail a ranch hand leading a white-faced roan out of the stables. 'Bring Misty over here! Miss McGuire needs a gentle mount, so you'll have to find another one for this afternoon.'

'I didn't m-mean now exactly,' Coley stuttered as Jase stepped down off his blood-bay stallion. Jase accepted the reins from the rider and turned to Coley.

'What's wrong with now?' His eyes twinkled wildly although the deadpan expression on his face didn't change.

'He's got you now,' Danny hooted, overcome with malicious brotherly glee at his sister's predicament.

'Nothing, except I promised Aunt Willy...' Coley began, searching wildly for some way out of the trap that her big mouth had got her into.

'There isn't anything that Aunt Willy would have for you that couldn't be put off,' Jase interrupted. Then he turned to the roan and stroked its neck. 'She just doesn't like you, Misty.'

'Oh, she's fine. I mean, she's ... there's nothing wrong with her. It's just ...'

'You'd better tell her yourself, because I don't think she believes me,' said Jase, shaking his head in mock despair.

Feeling like an utter fool, Coley stepped over towards the horse. Unwillingly she stared into the liquid brown eyes of the roan that blinked so trustingly back at her. As if on cue, the horse stepped forward and nuzzled Coley's shoulder until Coley placed a reluctant hand on its head and began stroking it.

'Misty likes you,' Jase commented, while Danny stood back, silently shaking with ill-concealed humour. 'Just a few turns around the corral wouldn't do any harm.'

'Oh, all right,' Coley agreed, slightly ashamed of her reluctance. She turned a glowering eye on her brother. 'But I don't need an audience.'

'I'll take my cue,' Danny grinned, and moved off towards the stables with a wave and a dubious 'good luck' to Jase.

'Okay. Now what?' Coley asked. Her anger was bolstering her courage.

'Come over here to the left side of the horse,' Jase instructed, taking her by the hand as he spoke.

'Do you have to get on from this side?' stalled Coley.

'It's best. It's the side that the horse is used to seeing a rider approach, so if you come from the other side he won't be expecting you and might spook,' he explained patiently.

'I thought a horse wouldn't let you get on him except from the one side.'

'No, that's not true. In fact, the Indians mounted their ponies on the opposite side,' Jase smiled. 'That peculiar quirk of theirs saved a cavalry patrol from ambush once.'

'Really?' Coley asked, interested in spite of herself.

79

'Two patrols were supposed to link up at a designated point. The scout from one patrol spotted the second patrol waiting for them. He was just going to report to his commanding officer that he had sighted the other patrol when he saw one of the so-called soldiers mount his horse—from the wrong side. He realized immediately that Indians must have wiped out the other patrol, stolen their uniforms and were waiting to ambush his patrol,' Jase concluded. He stared down at her rapt face. 'But that little story isn't getting you on this horse, and that's what we're supposed to be doing.'

Coley grinned at him shyly, and surprisingly he returned the smile. He threw the reins over the roan's head and turned back to Coley.

'Step over here,' he said, indicating a place on the ground at the horse's side. 'Place your right hand on the saddle horn and with your left hand grip the reins and rest your hand on the horse's neck.' He guided her hands through the moves. 'You always want to shorten the inside rein just a little so that the horse's head turns towards you. Never turn your back to the horse. Keep him in sight so that you know what he's doing. We have a few that take a playful nip here and there, or shy away when you try to mount.' He glanced at her to make sure she was taking it all in. 'All right, now place your left foot in the stirrup.'

Coley did as she was told, although her balance was not too good. Luckily the roan wasn't a big horse and Coley was fairly tall.

'Okay, now pull yourself into the saddle,' Jase finished.

It was a simple instruction, but not easy to carry out, as Coley soon discovered. She got halfway up, only to lose her balance and slip to the ground. She glanced at Jase and tried again. This time she got her leg over the saddle, straddled above it awkwardly for a second before receiving a shove from Jase that slipped her into the seat. She sat very still, her left hand clutching the saddle horn as well as her right, and stared down at the ground so very far below her. If Jase noticed the little waves of panic that were numbing her, he made no mention of them. He stepped to the roan's head, took hold of the reins under the chin, still retaining a hold on his own horse's reins and began walking. His voice was very matter-of-fact when he began speaking again.

'I'll lead you over to the corral so you can get used to the movement of the horse,' he said. 'All you have to do is relax, don't hold your body too rigid and follow the motion of the horse.'

Coley stared at a point between the horse's ears and tried to do as she was told. It sounded so simple. Jase stopped at the corral gate, opened it, and led the group in, closing the gate behind them. He swung easily into his saddle and reined his horse over beside Coley. He reached over and removed Coley's hands from the saddle horn, his eyes twinkling as she swallowed nervously. He placed the reins in her left hand and instructed her to let her other arm fall to her side. Against her better judgement, she did as she was told.

He showed her how to lay the reins against the side of the horse's neck to get him to turn, the proper length of rein from the horse's mouth to her hands, and, most important as far as Coley was concerned, how to stop him.

'We'll walk around the corral now. Just squeeze your legs and heels a bit.' He waited until she did it

81

before starting his own horse out.

After several plodding rounds, Coley felt quite good. She even relaxed a little. Of course, the ground wasn't quite as far away now, or at least it didn't seem to be.

'Do you want to try a trot?' Jase asked. She nodded confidently. 'Do the same as before, squeeze your legs.'

She did. Her horse began shuffling his feet in a lazy semblance of a trot while Coley bounced all over the saddle and nearly off. Instinctively she pulled her horse back into a walk. Her hazel eyes were very round when she looked over to Jase.

'This time, sit well back in the saddle so you don't get the motion of both the front and back legs of the horse. Don't move against the motion, ride with it. Try it again,' he said.

She'd gone too far to quit now, Coley thought, and resolutely tightened her legs against the horse's sides and off they went. She really tried to do as he said and succeeded to a certain extent, but she still bounced, although not quite as bad. Around and around the corral they went, Jase holding back his bay to stay along side the slow, shuffling roan.

'Let's canter now,' he ordered, and held back again until Coley had urged her horse to the faster pace.

'That's easy!' Coley exclaimed delightedly as Jase rode along side. The rhythmic, rocking motion was such a snap after the bouncing, jarring trot. 'This is fun!'

He pulled his horse into the centre of the corral and stopped. He watched her circle several times before he called to her that that was all for today. She pulled the roan up and turned him into the centre towards Jase.

'You've had enough for today. Any more riding and you'll be stiff as a board,' he smiled, and Coley smiled back. 'I'll tell the boys that Misty is yours. You can ride her whenever you like, but only in the corral for the next week or so until you get used to it.'

'Thanks,' Coley cried, rubbing the side of the roan's neck happily. She slid out of the saddle to the ground, leading her new mount over to the fence with Jase following suit. 'I never thought I could ride. I always got so frightened. But you didn't give me a chance.'

'That was the general idea,' he replied, leaning against a fence post.

'Still, I want to thank you. You've taught me to swim. Though I don't know how yet, I know I'm going to learn. And you've now taught me to ride,' Coley trailed off breathlessly. Then she glanced over at him with a sudden stab of guilt. 'I'm sorry about the way I behaved this morning. At the pool, I mean.'

'Nothing happened at the pool this morning,' Jase said coldly, turning his head to Coley where her gaze subsequently rested on his scar. 'Except in Tony's imagination.'

'I didn't mean that,' said Coley, lowering her head to watch her boot scuff the dirt of the corral. 'I meant that I didn't mean to make things more difficult for you.'

'How could you do that?' he asked, eyeing her speculatively.

'Well,' Coley's face was red now as she struggled over the words, 'I know you're in some sort of awkward position here on the ranch. I don't know why, only that it's something about your brother, and I don't want to do anything that would make things harder for you.' She searched his inscrutable face for some sign of understanding. 'You've been so good to me, teaching me things and all, that I don't want to get you in trouble over it.'

'I won't,' Jase answered, staring down at her with a very grim expression on his face. Seeing the anxious eyes dwelling on him, he smiled. 'So don't worry about me, my little yellow rose.'

Coley laughed and joined in step as he started towards the corral gate.

'You know you're really a very good teacher,' she smiled up at him. 'I can just see you teaching your sons and daughters.'

Her imagination painted bright little pictures as she spoke, of dark-haired little boys with blue eyes.

'There won't be any!' His voice was cold and hard. The biting tone brought Coley to a complete halt as she stared into his cold eyes filled with contempt. 'Because there won't be any wife.'

'Why ever not?' Coley asked. Her eyes grew round and just a trifle fearful at the anger and coldness in his face.

'I have nothing to offer a wife. Not a home, not a future, not an inheritance for children. Nothing!' Jase exclaimed bitterly. Coley stared at his cheek where the jagged scar seemed to be throbbing the rapid pulse of his temper. His hand reached up and touched the scar lightly with his fingertips. 'I have this for my wife,' he mocked. 'The mark of Cain.'

And he was gone while Coley stood silently within the backlash of his words.

CHAPTER FIVE

COLEY paddled idly in the water, enjoying the refreshing coolness of the pool in the afternoon sun. She could swim now, after a fashion, thanks to a week of intensive lessons from Jase. Of course, she had been restricted, like a child, to the shallow end of the pool whenever she swam alone. She could handle Misty pretty well now, too, but there again he wouldn't let her ride alone except in the corral. She grimaced disgustedly.

He treated her so differently. He had become distant and aloof since that first riding lesson. It was as if she was a total stranger. And all because of her big mouth, Coley thought. He had left yesterday to go into San Antoine for something or other and she hadn't even known he was going or even gone until she asked where he was at the dinner table last night. He could have at least said good-bye.

Depressed and hurt, Coley climbed out of the pool and began briskly rubbing her long legs and arms. She was too sensitive. How many times had Jase told her that? Well, he was too insensitive!

'Hi, golden girl,' said Tony, walking up behind Coley and plucking the swim cap from her head. 'What are you doing out here all by yourself? Don't you know two's company?'

'Aunt Willy and Uncle Ben are resting; Danny's out tinkering with his car, and Jase is gone. I was too hot to sit around sticking to chairs,' Coley remarked lightly. 'Where were you?'

'Would you believe I was looking for you?' Tony asked, taking the towel from Coley and drying off her back. At her mocking glance, he continued, 'It's true, I figured you'd probably be down riding your little merry-go-round.'

He handed Coley the towel back, his hand touching the golden tan of her shoulders.

'It was too hot for riding,' she replied lightly, ignoring his jibe. 'What did you want to see me for?'

'Danny needs some part for his car and I volunteered to go into town after it. I wondered if you wanted to ride along.'

'I'd like to,' Coley smiled, then flushed under the penetrating inspection of his black eyes. 'Give me a minute to change.'

'Not too long, princess,' Tony called after the rapidly departing Coley. When she was out of earshot, he added quietly, 'I'd like you all to myself.'

Coley changed quickly into a culotte shift, spent a few minutes touching up her make-up, and another few minutes arranging the soft curls of her now sunstreaked hair into flattering waves around her angular face. Skipping down the stairs to meet Tony, she reflected over the increasing attentiveness that Tony had been giving her. Ever since the day he had discovered her in Jason's arms in the pool, he had been watching her with a certain gleam in his eyes that had made her increasingly aware of him as more than just Ben's nephew.

'The golden pumpkin awaits you in the drive, Cinderella,' Tony teased, taking her arm possessively as she walked out the door on to the porch.

She smiled at him coyly as he opened the door of the gold and brown Cadillac and helped her inside. She was suddenly bursting with confidence again over her new looks, enjoying the compliments Tony's eyes kept sending.

The trip into town hardly seemed to take any time at all, what with the lively conversation that Tony kept up as he teased Coley into bursts of laughter with his outrageous remarks. She was so involved with her first active participation in flirting that she was only half conscious of the reckless speeds they were attaining. All too soon Tony pulled up in front of the store and hopped out, promising to be back in a jiffy. Coley leaned back against the plush cushions of the seat and gazed dreamily out of the window. She had just begun to wonder idly where Jase was and what he was doing when Tony opened the car door and tossed a package in the back seat before sliding in behind the wheel.

'Told you I wouldn't be long,' he said, turning the key in the ignition and manoeuvring the car into the street. 'Let's go to the drive-in and get a mug of cold, cold root beer, huh?'

'Sounds great,' Coley agreed.

'What were you thinking about a minute ago?' Tony asked, after they had parked in one of the stalls and he had given their order to one of the waitresses.

'When?'

'When I got in the car. You were all dreamy-eyed. Am I expecting too much to think that you just might have been thinking of me?' He gazed at her intently, though his lips were curved in a brilliant smile.

'Conceited,' Coley teased. 'Actually I was wondering about Jase.'

'Jase?' His narrow forehead creased into a scowl as he spat out the words in disbelief. 'What were you thinking about him for?'

Surprised by his nearly bitter tone, Coley stuttered in reply, 'I ... I knew he went to ... to San Antoine and I w-was just wondering where he was. Danny and I used to live there, that's all.'

'I'd forgotten,' Tony replied, as near an apology as he was capable of. He glanced at his watch. 'I imagine he's lying beside some pool with some sharp, bikinied beauty.'

'Does he have a girl-friend?' Coley asked, her spirits sinking with the picture that Tony had conjured in her mind.

'I imagine he has several,' Tony answered slyly, 'but not the kind you'd bring home to mother. Surely you didn't think he was some kind of a monk, did you, Coley?'

'No, of course not,' she replied, but with just enough uncertainty in her voice to make Tony chuckle maliciously.

'Coley, sometimes you're so darned naïve that I just can't believe it.' At the quick rising of colour in her cheeks, he reached over and held her hand. 'My sweet little Cinderella, not everyone is as inexperienced and pure as you are.' His voice grew husky as he continued, 'You just don't know how beautiful and tempting you are.'

The intensity etched on his slender face frightened her and she was glad when the waitress arrived with their drinks and Tony was forced to let go of her hands. As she accepted the frosty mug from him, she turned ever so slightly in her seat until she was resting against the door and had placed more distance between them.

'Did I embarrass you, princess?' Tony mocked, his arm nonchalantly over the back of the seat.

'Of course not,' Coley replied indignantly, now that she had recovered some of her composure. 'I don't see why you all seem to want to wrap me up in a package marked "Fragile". I am almost twenty.' Quickly the picture flashed in her mind of the night when she had asserted her womanhood to Jase and met his indifferent glance.

'Surely you can't accuse me of doing that?' Tony mocked.

'Yes, I can. You're just like all the rest,' she replied, enjoying the surge of righteous anger. 'You treat me like a child who has all the decisions made for her.'

'Now how do we do that?' Tony tilted his head and studied her with interest.

'Just look at all this secrecy with Jase,' Coley told him, leaning forward as she strived to make Tony understand. 'Everyone knows what happened—about his scar and his brother, I mean. Everybody, but me. Every time I ask someone they just pat me on the head and tell me to run along like a good little girl.'

Tony laughed lightly at her indignant words, but his eyes had narrowed into two glittering black dots. 'What could it possibly accomplish for someone to tell you that? It's water under the bridge, so to speak.'

'Then how come Danny knows?' she flared.

'Maybe you're right, princess.' His expression grew serious as he studied her before he turned to stare out the front of the car. 'You're one of the family now. You should know what happened.'

'Will you tell me, Tony?' Coley asked breathlessly.

He didn't answer her for a minute, just stared at her

sombrely.

'I don't really know where to begin.' He frowned slightly and swirled the root beer in his mug. 'Rick, his brother, was two years older than Jase. He was some kind of guy.' Tony smiled briefly. 'I think you would have liked him, Coley. He was kinda crazy, always ready to do anything, try anything. Just the opposite of Jase. But Rick was Uncle Ben's favourite. It didn't matter what Rick wanted to do or where he wanted to go, it was okay with Ben. Anyway, one night Rick came home late. He'd been to a party and he'd been drinking pretty heavily.' Tony paused and glanced over at Coley. He seemed to hesitate. 'Nobody knows for sure what happened from here on. We do know Rick went into the pen with Satan, that big Brahma bull we've got out there. Rick was forever teasing him, jumping in and out of the pen like a rodeo clown. He wasn't so lucky that night. The booze had affected his reflexes and the bull got him. Jase said he heard the commotion and came out. He eventually got Rick out of the pen, but not before Satan had gored Rick and slashed Jason's cheek with his horns.

'Uncle Ben wasn't paralysed then. I saw him sitting on the ground holding Rick in his arms, tears streaming down his face. I'll never forget the sight of him crying like a baby. I don't know where Jase was, calling an ambulance, I guess. Rick was still conscious.' Tony's voice became strained. Coley huddled in the sunshine beating through the window, shivering in spite of the warmth. 'He was delirious. He kept screaming for Jase, crying, "He's going to get me. . . . Don't just stand there, help me!" I guess he kept that up all the way to the hospital, with the old man breaking up beside him and Jase just sitting stone-faced through the whole thing. Rick died on the operating table.

'There was an inquest after his death,' Tony went on. 'During his testimony, Jase said that he couldn't have got Rick out of the pen any quicker than he did. That was when Ben went to pieces, shouting that Jase was a liar and a murderer, that he'd let his brother die because he knew Rick would inherit the ranch. He swore that Jase had deliberately stayed outside the pen and watched his brother being gored to death. Jase never said a word. He just let the old man rage on until he told Jase that he would carry the mark of Cain for the rest of his life. Then he walked out and the old man collapsed with a stroke. He's been in a wheelchair ever since.'

A pregnant silence followed the conclusion of Tony's words that not even the outside noises of the drive-in seemed to penetrate. Finally Tony looked over at the white face beside him.

'Now you know. Aren't you glad?' His voice was bitter as he pushed impatiently on the horn for the attendant to pick up the tray.

Coley didn't reply. She didn't speak the rest of the way home. She just sat and stared out the window at the blur of the scenery. When they finally reached the ranch house, she crawled out of the car and hurried straight for her room where she lay on the bed staring numbly at the bright flowers on the wall.

The lone horse and rider stood silently within the corral, both gazing over the rails at the distant, shimmering hills. The horse whinnied forlornly. Coley sighed in agreement while rubbing her horse's neck affectionately.

91

'I know. I wish we could go riding out there, but you know what Jase said, Misty,' she concluded with a wistful but resigned expression on her face.

She had been in a rather melancholy mood since Tony had told her the story of Rick's death three days ago. Jase was back from his trip to San Antoine, but Coley had been reluctant to be alone with him. Not that Tony's story had outright damned Jase. She still instinctively trusted him, but she recognized that there existed a slightly ruthless side to his nature.

'Hey, little princess, want to take that rocking horse of yours for a ride?'

Coley turned around in the saddle to see Tony astride a prancing chestnut horse at the corral gate. She reined her horse around and trotted it over to him.

'I'm not supposed to go out of the corral. Besides, aren't you supposed to be working?' she asked. For some reason, despite her earlier expressed desire for a ride in the country, she didn't really want to go with Tony.

'Another one of Jase's edicts?' he mocked with a sarcastic curl of his upper lip. 'Or don't you think you'd be safe with me?'

'Why would I think a thing like that?' Coley protested, her conscience feeling a twinge of guilt. 'Jase just didn't want me going out by myself. And if you're going to be working, I don't want to be in the way.'

'You won't be,' Tony remarked as he reached down and unlatched the gate. With difficulty, he manoeuvred his high-spirited mount into a position to swing the gate open. 'Jase wants me to check the well up on the north range. It's another one of his fool's errands, so you might as well keep me company,'

Tony grimaced, reining his horse over to Coley's side.

'Why do you say that?'

'With all the rain we've had, there's more than enough water for the horses up there,' he grumbled, 'but he's sending me anyway.'

Coley wasn't in the mood to take part in any discussion about Jase, so she nudged her horse into a canter. Tony's jumping chestnut was soon alongside. She flinched as she watched him saw at the reins, his horse's mouth opened wide.

'Misty and I were just wishing we could go out riding,' she remarked, trying to turn her attention away from the flecks of blood that dotted the saliva foaming around the horse's mouth.

'Then I'm glad Jase dreamed up this little chore for me. I'm getting my wish to be with you and you're getting yours to go riding.' He smiled broadly while his eyes roamed over her face in open admiration.

Coley's cheeks flushed at his words. Tony seemed pleased by her reaction and turned his attention to the rolling landscape with a satisfied smile curling the corners of his mouth. Coley glanced around with interest. It was her first venture on to the ranch proper since her dismal trek the night of the storm. The tranquil beauty of the hills and distant mountains seemed far removed from the sinister and ominous shapes the lightning had revealed. They rode several miles with only subdued exclamations from Coley at the sight of giant yucca plants, their stalks rounded with clusters of blossoms. Occasionally Tony would catch her attention to point out the white rumps of antelopes bounding away at their approach. When he finally slowed his horse to a walk, it was a wide-eyed and breathless rider that reined in beside him, her eyes dancing with pleasure and delight.

'Oh, that was so much fun!' Coley exclaimed. 'You are so lucky to be able to ride all over.'

'I'm enjoying it today, but most days it's a bore,' he replied, reining his horse into a ravine. 'What do you see right now?'

The sides of the ravine sloped away to reveal a canyon meadow with a thin ribbon of sparkling water slicing it in two. On the rich dark grasses grazed a herd of horses. At the entrance to the canyon, the two riders halted: A frolicsome colt kicked his heels and dashed in whickering panic to the safety of his mother's side at their appearance.

'We have one of the best studs in the state. His ancestry, on both sides, traces directly back to Old Sorrel, one of the founding sires of the Quarter Horse breed. Those are Sun God's colts and fillies out there with one of our herd stallions. You can bet they'd fetch a high price in any auction,' Tony told her, his eyes never leaving the herd before them.

Coley studied the foals as they peeped around their mothers' sides while the bolder ones skirmished playfully with each other. Each one seemed a replica of the other, from their red-gold coats to their flaxen mane and tails down to the white stockings on their feet and the blaze on their faces.

'They all look alike.'

'That's what makes Sun God such a valuable stallion. He breeds true, just like Old Sorrel did,' Tony explained, 'Old Sorrel was born and raised down on the famous King Ranch near Alice, Texas.'

'You're very lucky to know so much about all this.' Coley glanced at him briefly before turning back to the herd. 'How long have you lived here?'

'I came here seven years ago, after my father died. I was sixteen then,' said Tony, lightly touching a spur to his horse's flank as they moved out together at a walk. 'My mother was Ben's baby sister. If you can picture a female version of Ben, that was my mother.' His smile as he glanced over at Coley was scornful. 'She was already an old maid when she ran away with my father. Poor Dad, he worked here on the ranch for Ben. He figured by marrying Ben's sister he'd have it made. Of course, he didn't know Ben too well. He threw them both off the ranch. I came along a few years later. From the time I can remember, Mom was a regular shrew, constantly reminding Dad of all the things she'd had, and it was all his fault that we lived in such squalor. I was twelve when she flew into her final rage and her heart burst under the constant strain. And Dad, who only wanted an easy life, spent fifteen years of hell with her. But he never stopped trying. He got involved smuggling drugs across the border and was fatally wounded in a gun battle with Treasury agents. Even on his deathbed, his last words were that this ranch was my heritage and for me to claim my share. Since I was a minor, the court declared Ben my guardian and I came here. Not a happy story, is it?' Tony smiled grimly at Coley, his dark eyes studying her face intently. At the short, negative shake of her head, he added, 'But from what Danny's told me, yours isn't pretty either. We're a lot alike, Coley.'

A lump in her throat prevented her from replying. Poor, proud Tony, she thought; he always seemed so carefree, teasing her and constantly attempting to charm her into gaining more self-confidence and his life had been harder than her own. How mean of her to think badly of him when he teased her. He was trying to help her fit in, to be a part of the family. She blinked hastily at the tears forming in her eyes. It wouldn't do for Tony to see her pity.

She didn't notice the calculating gleam in his eye as he studied her face.

'Look at this view, Coley,' he directed, sweeping a hand around him.

She looked around her in surprise. During their slow ride around the herd, they had climbed the crest of the canyon. Spread out below them were the coppery forms of the horses peacefully grazing on the canyon floor. Shimmering in the distance were the tiny toy buildings of the ranchyard. Behind them were the craggy hills and mountains. Dark splotches of cattle dotted the pastures between the ranch house and the canyon.

'As far as the eye can see is Slash S rangeland,' Tony said calmly but forcefully. 'All told, over sixty square miles, valued, with livestock and all, in the millions. And now it looks like one day it will all be mine.' He turned once again to Coley. 'You know, Ben's grown very fond of you these few short weeks you've been here. He told Willy your gentle ways hid a lot of determination and pride.' Coley's eyes were captured by the forcefulness of his gaze. 'I feel I have to warn you Jase realizes that Ben likes you. He's not above using you as a tool to get it. He constantly tries to make me look bad, gives me menial tasks, like today, then implies to Ben that I can't be trusted. He wants this ranch, Coley, any way he can get it.'

On that ominous note Tony stopped, turning a grim face towards the hills. Jase's words came echoing back to Coley. 'Tony would destroy everything you worked for in a week.'

Very hesitantly Coley spoke. 'But if what you told me the other day is true, about Rick's death, isn't the ranch rightly his?'

There was a long silence during which it seemed Tony was choosing his words carefully before he answered.

'Nobody saw what happened. We have only the version Jase told us and the barely lucid cries of Rick while he was conscious but delirious. Rick was very clear when he begged Jase not to stand there ... to help him.'

'What if someone else were there?'

His gaze sharpened as he studied her face.

'What if the sight of three thousand pounds of charging Brahma bull momentarily froze Jase? What if the horror inside the corral stopped him?' Tony asked, his complexion paling under his tan.

'Is that what you believe?' Coley asked breathlessly, half afraid to hear his answer.

'It's possible. That's what Ben believes,' Tony answered calmly, lifting his eyebrows briefly in an almost indifferent shrug. 'That and the fact that Jase wanted the ranch, which will now, quite likely, be mine.' Suddenly he smiled at her, his thin lips curling back to reveal a large expanse of white teeth. 'How did we get on such a morbid subject when we both were enjoying the ride? *Quien sabe*, huh? I'll tell you what, you stay here and watch the colts play while I ride over the hill and check the pump on that water well.'

Coley nodded a quick agreement. She needed time to be alone, to think about Tony's new revelations. She smiled and waved in return as his horse danced down the hill. Her eyes followed him until he was out of sight. With a barely repressed sigh, Coley dismounted, leading her horse part way down the crest to a grassy level spot where she let loose of the reins to allow Misty to graze. She stretched out on the incline, leaning back to gaze up at the vivid blue sky.

How strange that she had never guessed that Tony's occasional brashness had come from an unhappy childhood. She remembered often seeing those same lines of bitterness and discontent etched on Danny's face before they had come here. In some ways the circumstances of Tony's early life had been like theirs, except that he never had known a mother's love and possibly not even a father's.

Her brows constricted briefly. She wished they had not talked about Jase. So many things Tony had said seemed logical, though in direct conflict with her emotions. She had recognized the flash of ruthlessness occasionally revealed in Jase's face. Perhaps there was cruelty there as well. Coley rolled over quickly on her side as if to turn her back on such thoughts.

A movement several feet away caught her attention. Misty's front hoof had stepped on one of the trailing reins causing her to stumble. Coley leapt quickly to her feet.

'Oh, Misty, I'm sorry!' she cried, rushing over to pat the roan's neck soothingly. 'I should have realized you'd trip over the reins. Here, I'll tie them around the saddle horn.'

Finishing her task, she stepped back to watch her horse lower its head to the tender mountain grasses, unencumbered by loose reins. A questioning whinny rang from the canyon floor. The roan's head raised and her ears pricked alertly as she stared down. Her sides heaved briefly in an answering whicker.

'Have you got a friend down there, Misty?' Coley asked, studying the numerous horses, trying to determine which one had called to her horse.

Misty whinnied again, then started down the slope at an eager trot.

'Where are you going?' Coley cried. 'Come back here! Misty!'

She hopped and slid down the steep incline to the canyon floor, vainly attempting to catch up with her unheeding horse. She was barely halfway down when Misty reached the bottom and cantered towards the herd.

'Misty! Misty!' Coley called, trying desperately to run after her horse and still maintain her balance. Her feet failed to keep up with her gathering momentum and she landed ignominiously on her rump. She rolled and slid to the bottom, scraping and bruising her arms and hands as she tried to stop her fall. Out of breath and painfully sore, she struggled to her feet and hobbled stiffly after her roan. But Misty had reached the herd. There was a brief flurry of movement before the curious mares encircled the saddled but riderless horse and she was hidden from Coley's view.

'Oh, Misty, how could you do this to me!' Coley exclaimed disgustedly, slowing down to a disgruntled, toe-scuffling walk.

From the grove of trees that lined the opposite canyon walls came a shrill, almost whistle-like sound followed almost immediately by a thundering of hooves. Coley glanced up quickly from her morose study of the ground to see a coppery red horse charging around the herd towards her. While the mares and colts scurried together, the sorrel horse slowed to a dancing halt between Coley and the herd. With long powerful strides he paced back and forth in front of her, his flaxen tail held high, flowing out behind him like a banner going into battle. Coley paused, then chided herself for the momentary recurrence of her fear of horses. She clapped her hands loudly and stepped boldly forward.

'Shoo, horse, shoo!' she yelled, flapping her arms, wildly, hoping to send him scurrying off.

His shrill, piercing scream sent her hands rushing to cover her ears as he, snakelike, lowered his head, snorting loudly and stamping the ground. Coley realized with growing terror that he wasn't a bit afraid of her and had no intention of allowing her to approach the herd he was protecting. She glanced around her hopelessly. All the trees of any size were on the opposite side of the canyon. Ahead of her and slightly to her right was a huge boulder where, if she could make it and scramble up it, she would be out of reach of her angry antagonist. Now her dilemma was should she try for it, stand her ground or retreat. The last two left her more vulnerable to him if he decided she posed a threat wherever she was. That only left the first, to try for the rock.

Taking a deep breath, Coley tried to still the trembling in her legs. They felt like two sticks of jelly. The horse was tossing his head, shaking it from side to side. Now, she thought, now! And she was off, the ground shuddering beneath her as the pounding of the horse's hooves foretold without the need of a glance that he was giving chase.

She was at the rock! She made it! Scrambling, clawing, inwardly cursing the slick soles of her cowboy boots, she dragged herself to the top. The angry screams and clicking teeth below her underlined the fine line separating defeat from her victory. Coley tucked her legs beneath her as she clung tightly to the pointed top of her precarious perch. Below danced the sorrel, rearing and pawing in a tantrum.

'Help!' Her voice was barely a squeak. She swallowed hard and tried again. 'Help!'

Tony wasn't far away. Surely he'd hear her.

'Help! Tony, help!'

The enraged stallion circled the boulder, his fiery eyes never leaving his quarry.

She watched the slope she had just come down, fervently hoping to see Tony appear on the crest.

'To-o-ne-ee!' She screamed at the top of her lungs, before breaking off into a hastily stifled sob.

She mustn't panic. The horse couldn't reach her and Tony would be along soon. She just had to keep her head. 'Take deep breaths,' she ordered her body. 'Relax. Enjoy the view.' After all, all she had to do was wait. She glanced down at the horse, trying to be calm, but she couldn't suppress a shudder at the sight of the bared and menacing teeth.

A muffled sound of hoofbeats reached her ears, but they seemed to be coming from the opposite side of the canyon, from the hill that was its wall. Seconds later a horse and rider appeared on the crest above the grove of trees. The horse pranced impatiently against the backdrop of blue sky, as Coley, holding her breath, stared at the rider. Even at this distance she recognized the calm way he sat so surely astride the dancing red horse, moving with his mount as if they were one. It was Jase.

'Jase! Jase!' Coley screamed, waving an arm frantically at him.

What if he didn't see her?

The horrifying thought numbed her throat as she rose precariously to her feet trying to balance herself astride the pointed rock.

'Here! Here! I'm over here!' she yelled. Again she waved her arm wildly.

Suddenly the slick soles could no longer maintain their hold and she slipped. A short cry escaped her lips as she clutched madly at the smooth boulder trying to check her fall. She felt her blouse rip as a corner snagged on a small outcropping. Quickly she grabbed at the small hold. Straining every muscle in her slender arms, she managed to stop her slide. Without wasting a glance to see where the stallion was, because she could amost feel the heat of his breath on her, she began to scale the rock again. A glancing blow of a hoof struck the heavy though slick sole of her boot, adding impetus to her scramble to safety. Completely winded, she reached the top, tears streaming down her cheeks from fright.

Her hazel eyes lifted to the hill where she had seen Jase, but he was gone. Suddenly she realized that pounding noise she was hearing wasn't her heart as she had first thought, but a horse. She turned to see Tony plummeting down the slope, yelling and spurring his horse, his arm swinging a coiled rope wildly.

Momentarily the stallion below paused as if preparing to meet the attack before he spun and raced whinnyingly towards the herd. In an almost synchronized movement, the whole herd turned as one and raced from the canyon, the copper sorrel nipping at the heels of the stragglers.

Tony slid his horse to a stop at the base of the rock where Coley was perched. He dismounted quickly to rush over to help her down. His face was as pale as hers, except that his expression was triumphant and hers was relieved.

'Are you all right?' he asked, smiling down at her broadly.

Coley nodded, not trusting her voice at the moment. She glanced once again at the hill where she had seen Jase. But still there was no sign of him. Had she imagined it? Tony was speaking again and she turned back to him, her hands resting on his arms.

'I was so afraid something would happen to you, too,' he said, a tightness in his voice. 'Where's your horse?'

'She ran out with the herd.' Coley's voice trembled. She was still so shaken by her close call that she had difficulty concentrating, and speaking. 'Oh, Tony, I'm so glad to see you!'

'You just lean back against the rock and relax. We'll worry about catching up with your horse later. Right now I'll take a look at those hands.'

Coley did as she was ordered, wincing as he dabbed at the grazes in her hands with his handkerchief.

'They're just minor. We'll wash them good when we get back to the ranch,' he said, his dark eyes returning to her face.

She glanced down at her hands in a daze. The ragged strands of her torn blouse flipped outwards at a gentle stir of wind. Instantly her hands raised to hide her breasts barely covered by her lacy bra. Her gaze lifted hesitantly to his, discomfitingly aware of her reddening face.

'It's nice to see a girl blush.' Tony's eyes sparkled as he lightly touched her cheek with his hand.

Then his expression changed to a rather lazy regard

of her face, as his arms moved into position, one on each side of her.

'Isn't it usual for a damsel to reward her knight with a kiss?' he asked huskily. His tanned face moved in closer to hers. 'Or haven't your lips ever touched a man's before?'

As his face lowered towards hers, the ugly picture of another such scene flashed before Coley. Before it had been Carl, now it was Tony, but the feeling of repulsion was the same.

'*No!*' she shouted vehemently, squirming out of his grasp.

'I wasn't going to bite you!' he exclaimed in stunned disbelief.

Instantly Coley was contrite.

'I'm sorry, Tony. I didn't mean to ... I guess I'm still uptight.' The words came slowly through the invisible stranglehold of fear and tension around her throat.

'Of course,' Tony agreed. His stiff expression relaxed slightly. 'We'd better get you home.'

He turned, gathered up the reins and mounted his horse. 'Here,' he held out his hand to her. 'You can ride up front.'

Clutching the shredded edges of her blouse together as best she could with one hand, Coley placed the other in his. Rather ungracefully she hopped and was pulled on to the horse. Tony's arm encircled her waist, nearly bared by the torn blouse. She tried to quell the feeling of discomfort. After all, it was too far to walk home.

CHAPTER SIX

COLEY and Tony had ridden only twenty yards out of the ravine that led to the canyon when Jase appeared leading Coley's horse.

So she had seen him on that ridge after all!

His eyes were afire with blue flames burning their brightest when they rested on Coley. His face darkened like a thundercloud, his scar a jagged white lightning bolt.

'I see Tony rescued you in one piece—or almost,' he added, his glance flickering over Coley's blouse.

'It tore on the rock,' she said quickly. A rush of warmth covered her face at his derisive and accusing glance.

'How convenient. Your horse has been trained to stay when the reins hang to the ground. It's called ground-hitching,' Jase explained with sarcastic preciseness. 'To tie the reins to the saddle horn is an open invitation for the horse to leave.'

'Coley, you didn't!' hooted Tony. 'Of all the greenhorn...'

'That's enough!' Jase interrupted sharply.

Coley felt Tony stiffen behind her before slumping sullenly in the saddle.

'Was that pump working?'

'Yeah, it was,' Tony snapped. 'What were you doing? Riding over to check up on me?'

'Did you oil it?' Jase completely ignored Tony's

question and Tony ignored his. 'I said did you oil it?' he repeated in a darkly ominous voice.

'No.'

'Then go and do it. Coley, get down from there and put this on,' he ordered, reaching behind his saddle to untie his ever-present rain slicker.

'You go and check on it!' Tony fumed. 'I'm taking Coley back to the ranch.'

'You'll do as you're told,' Jase stated unequivocally.

Coley slid from the saddle and gratefully took the slicker from Jase's outstretched hand.

'You don't give all the orders around here,' Tony sneered.

'But I gave this one!'

Tony sat in the saddle, shaking with anger before digging the spurs into his horse and spinning him back in the direction of the canyon. Turning his head over his shoulder, he glared at Jase.

'My day will come,' he said darkly.

'You and I both know what would happen to this ranch if it ever did. You'd sell it to the first bidder. That's why I'll never let it happen,' Jase replied sharply.

With a sharp crack of the reins on his horse's rump Tony bounded away. Jase turned slowly to Coley, nearly drowning in the over-sized rain slicker. She couldn't meet his gaze squarely, so she shuffled over to her horse.

'Do you need help getting on?' he asked flatly.

'I can manage,' she replied, trying vainly to push back the sleeves so she could mount.

He set his horse off the' minute she was in the saddle. His horse was naturally faster gaited than her roan, so the entire ride to the ranch-yard was made with Coley trailing behind. The whole way Coley kept thinking all she had to do was say, 'Jase, why didn't you come down the hill to help me?' The words were so simple, why wouldn't they come out? But she knew the answer to that. Tony had implied very clearly that Jase had had cold feet on one other occasion. As much as she wished otherwise, Coley couldn't forget that. At the corral, she pulled her mount to a stop beside his blood bay.

'I'll have one of the boys take care of your horse. You go on up to the house and have Maggie take a look at your hands,' Jase ordered before reining his horse towards the stables.

Coley watched him glumly before swinging out of the saddle on to the ground. She flipped the reins over the corral fence with a quick half-hitch, then hurried to the house. No one was in the hallway when she entered, so she went immediately upstairs. She rolled the raincoat up and buried her torn blouse in the wastebasket, replacing it with a fresh one. She didn't feel like going into the details of what had happened. Ashamed of her thoughts against Jase and unwilling to have them spread before anyone else, she chose to make as little of the incident as possible.

On her way downstairs she left the raincoat in Jase's room. It would save having to face him in private.

The following day Coley was walking Misty around the corral when Jase rode up. She was so deep in thought over yesterday's happenings that, at first, she didn't notice him.

'How are your hands?' he asked, leaning an arm on his saddle horn while studying her intently.

'They're okay,' Coley replied as she glanced down

at them absently. Her heart seemed to be pounding in her throat.

'Come on. We're going for a ride,' Jase ordered.

He bent down and swung open the corral gate. Coley trotted her roan over to his side and followed meekly, though apprehensively, as he led the way through the ranch-yard into the pastures. She saw him glance at her curiously with a slightly bitter smile before he urged his horse into a canter.

Thank heaven she didn't have to talk to him yet. She didn't know what to say and she never was any good at talking about trivial things.

Gradually the landscape began to grow more and more familiar. With a mounting breathlessness and tension, Coley realized he was taking her back to the canyon. Sooner than she wanted, the ravine entrance appeared before them. But instead of heading towards it, Jase veered to the left. She glanced at him nervously, longing to ask where he was taking her while dreading to break the tense silence. In the next instant they were climbing the incline of the outer canyon wall, Coley following behind the ramrod-straight back.

At the top he reined his horse in and dismounted, indicating with a gesture that she should do the same. She complied reluctantly. She stood motionless as Jase led his horse across the crest to the inner canyon side. She watched him stop, cup a match to a cheroot before glancing back at her. With a sigh she walked forward. As she drew even with him, her eyes never leaving his still figure, he called out sharply, 'That's far enough!'

Coley stopped with a jerk, staring first ahead of her, then down. She felt the blood rush from her face. In front of her were the tops of the trees that lined this side of the canyon floor. But just two steps away was a sheer drop of over fifty feet. Then Jase was taking her arm and leading her away from the edge. Calmly he sat her down on the grassy crest, settling down himself two feet away.

Coley swallowed numbly. She should say something. He had obviously known that she had wondered why he hadn't come down yesterday to help her. Despite Tony's implication that Jase was a coward, Coley hadn't accepted that, but, before, she hadn't been able to come up with a logical explanation of why Jase didn't resuce her. Now she knew. He had fifty feet of reasons.

'I know I cleared up one question, but what else is bothering you?' Jase asked harshly. His blue eyes rested on her face, searching it relentlessly.

'Nothing,' she replied, none too positively.

'Something happened when I was in San Antoine, didn't it?' he went on.

Coley plucked a blade of grass nervously and watched it twirl in her fingers. She could feel his determination and she hesitated telling him the reason for her quietness.

'Coley.' His voice was low and threatening.

'Tony took me into town last Saturday,' she said finally, glancing at him briefly out of the corner of her eye.

'And?'

'And——' Coley paused. 'And he told me how Rick died.' She flinched as she saw Jason's dark head jerk back as if he'd been struck.

'I see,' he murmured as he leaned back on one elbow and stared at her with his diamond-sharp gaze.

'I asked him,' she asserted. An anger grew within

her at his withdrawal. 'I'm grown up. Things don't have to be hidden from me as if I were a child.'

'If you were grown up, Coley, you wouldn't have to keep reminding people,' Jase smiled cynically. 'Now that you know, what good has it done you?'

Coley shrugged.

'I don't know,' she said finally, 'but I do know that you couldn't be a coward any more than you could be a murderer.'

'Coley, for God's sake, grow up!' Jase exclaimed angrily. 'I'm not some knight in tarnished armour who needs a maiden to defend him!'

'You're not trying to make me believe that you could have saved Rick and didn't, are you?' Coley exclaimed. Painfully hurt by his anger, she jumped to her feet. 'Because if you are, I'm not going to believe you! I know you're not like that!'

He rose and stood silently behind her. 'Coley.' He watched as her slender shoulders shook with her silent sobs. His hands reached forward and drew her stiff back into his arms until his chin rested on her sun-streaked curls. 'It's true that I want this ranch more than anything in this world.'

With a heartrending sob, she wrenched herself free of his arms and ran to her horse. She was in the saddle and jerking the roan's head around when Jase caught hold of the bridle. She stared down at him, unashamed of the tears that were streaming down her cheeks.

'I told you you'd only be hurt,' Jase said quietly. His rugged features were set in a hard line and his eyes were bitter.

'Jason Savage, if you really believed all those things you said about yourself, you wouldn't be here now,'

110

Coley said through clenched teeth. 'And if you really want this ranch as much as you say you do, then you wouldn't care whose feet you'd have to kiss to get it nor what you'd have to do to prove you didn't let your brother die. But you haven't done either one. So I think you're just too proud. Too proud to go to your grandfather and tell him how you grieve for your brother and how you wish you could have got there sooner, and ... and ...'

She couldn't finish. She burst into tears and ended by jerking the roan out of his grasp. Viciously Coley put a heel to the horse's flank and raced down the hill, seeing nothing except the wall of water in front of her eyes.

She was in the ranch-yard unsaddling her horse when Jase finally trotted his horse in. He reined in beside her and watched silently as she fumbled with the cinch in a desperate attempt to ignore him.

'Well?' she finally said in exasperation, staring at him boldly.

'I was wondering if the thorns were still on my long-stemmed yellow rose.' His eyes gleamed down at her, bright and questioning.

'Yes, they are,' Coley replied angrily, pulling the heavy western saddle off the roan and dropping it on the ground.

'You can go ahead and ride alone from now on, as long as you stay within sight of the ranch and don't go near the pens.' He didn't need to spell out which pens; Coley knew he meant the Brahmas.

Only after he had turned his bay around and headed back out to the pastures did Coley stop to stare wistfully after him.

At the dinner table that evening Jase and Ben began bickering about the advisability of moving a herd of stock cattle out of the south section. Jase felt they should wait and Ben said he wanted it done now. Of late, these dinner-table discussions had usually become quite heated as both were stubbornly against giving in to each other. Coley listened to the exchange quite indifferently until Jase happened to glance her way. He stopped almost in mid-sentence as he studied her smug 'I-told-you-so' expression before flashing her an amused and intimate smile. Coley tingled under its bewitching warmth.

'Ben,' Jase turned his smile to the gnarled, grey-haired man at the head of the table, 'if you think I should move them, I will. Would you pass me some more of Maggie's bread?'

His sudden acquiescence startled Ben, but it did not mollify him in the slightest. He turned his scowling face towards Coley, who quickly lowered her gaze to her plate so that he wouldn't see the bubbly brightness on her face. Instead she quickly started a nonsensical conversation with her brother over an imaginary difficulty in bridling her horse. The meal ended with Coley in giggles over some of the ludicrous suggestions proposed by Danny and Tony.

Uncle Ben refused to join them on the porch, insisting that he had things to do in his study. Coley couldn't help thinking that he was doing a bit of childish sulking. Unconsciously she joined Jase on the cushioned porch swing and listened to Danny as he used his persuasive tactics on Tony to help him work on the transmission of his car. In the end Tony gave in, reluctantly, and followed Danny out into the yard, but not with the same amount of enthusiasm that

Danny had. Coley leaned back on the swing and gazed at the crimson-kissed clouds of the sunset while listening to the well-modulated voice of Jase as he talked to Aunt Willy about her very favourite subject, her roses.

'I was just mentioning to Colleen the other day that as soon as my tea roses bloom we should have a garden party,' Aunt Willy chattered, only to be interrupted by the distant shrill of the telephone in the house. 'My goodness, I wonder who that could be.'

Coley watched with an amused smile as her aunt rose quickly from her chair, unceremoniously tugging at her creeping skirt before dashing into the house after the persistent ring.

At the strike of a match from the man beside her, Coley turned her head to watch him light his familiar cheroot. A black eyebrow raised inquiringly at her. For a minute Coley studied him, admiring the strong, rugged angles of his face, the arrogant boldness of his nose, the soft yet cynical curl of his lips, the smooth, tanned forehead and the arching brows over his brilliant ice-blue eyes. The scar across his cheek seemed natural, a part of him, no longer frightening and ugly. Then the smoke from his cigar drifted between them, blurring her vision, and she turned again towards the sunset.

'What pearl of wisdom are you thinking of now?' he mocked lightly. 'Or did you run out of them this afternoon?'

'I was right, you know,' Coley replied, tilting her button nose upwards ever so slightly at his words. 'It takes two to make an argument. You proved that tonight at the table.'

'It wasn't really an argument, more like a difference of opinion,' Jase answered.

113

'It was rather a loud difference, then,' Coley said, accenting 'loud' with a trace of censure in her voice which earned her a quiet laugh from Jase.

'And you feel I did the right thing, agreeing to his decision?' he asked.

'Yes, I do. It's time you two stopped lashing out at each other, trying to draw the first blood. He's an old man, Jase,' Coley said earnestly. 'And he's crippled. He should be pitied and comforted, not quarrelled with.'

'He's a Savage,' retorted Jase angrily, 'and no Savage needs pity.'

'All right, compassion then,' Coley inserted quickly, feeling a little flare of temper herself. 'As much as you love this ranch, you should understand, of all people, how frustrating it must be to be confined to a wheelchair and not be able to get out and see what's going on. I believe you and your grandfather are equally devoted to this land.'

'The Slash S is Savage Land,' Jase declared, rising abruptly to his feet to lean against the porch railing and stare out over the darkening land. 'And as long as there's a Savage alive, I'll never stand by and watch it go to anyone else. I'll do anything to stop it.'

The passionate outburst brought Coley to her feet, moving her towards the straight back and broad shoulders at the rail. She stood silently beside him and laid a hand on the tanned arm that was gripping the wooden rail tensely. At her touch he turned and looked down at her.

'Do you really believe that Ben doesn't feel the same way about this land?' Coley asked. Her eyes were wide and anxious as she gazed up into his stern face.

114

Slowly he turned and placed his hands lightly on her shoulders. A softness returned to him as he looked at her.

'Coley, however right you may be,' his voice was low and husky, 'you can't wipe away the suspicion and distrust that has accumulated over a period of several years with a few words. There are some wounds that take more than a kiss to make them better. They take time. So don't push us too fast.' Very lightly he turned her around and gently pushed her towards the steps leading down on to the lawn. 'Now, run along and find out what your brother and Tony are doing.'

Reluctantly Coley stepped off the veranda, gazing back at Jase wistfully. He had lit another cigar and was watching the grey smoke as it drifted lazily in the night air. She turned her head and directed her unwilling feet away from the porch and Jase. She felt no elation or triumph, just a curious sense of suffering as if she had taken over part of his burden. But why was her heart beating so loudly and she was trembling too? Why?

With an impatient hand, Coley wiped away the beads of perspiration that had gathered on her forehead in the hot Texas sun as she fed the last of an apple to her horse. The heat had sapped the enjoyment out of her late afternoon ride, ending it much sooner than was usual. Lethargically she patted the roan's head and moved away, her boots scuffing at the scorched ground as she walked.

She sighed dejectedly as she glanced around the yard. She had thought Jase would be back by now. He had left the morning after their talk on the porch to move the cattle out of the south section. Everything seemed so purposeless without him around, and in this heat, there wasn't anything to do. Briefly Coley considered taking a short swim in the pool, but rejected it just as quickly. It would take more energy to change than she possessed right now. She didn't feel like going up to the house; she was too restless to sit around. So she just maintained her aimless, wandering pace.

Her fingers trailed lazily on the top rail of the fence as she meandered around the corrals glancing disinterestedly at their occupants. In front of her were the reinforced fences marking the Brahma cattle enclosures. A little gleam of curiosity directed her footsteps towards the pens and the heavy plank boards that hid them from her view. She stood on tiptoe to try to peer over the slats, but the fence was too tall. Putting her feet on the bottom rail, Coley hoisted herself up to rest her elbows on the top board.

The lone inhabitant was at the far end of the pen, but at the sound of Coley climbing on to the fence he had turned to face her. The heat waves shimmered eerily between them as the sun cast a ghostly grey sheen to his hide. The enormous size of the animal glued Coley to the fence, the grotesque hump on his shoulders and the loose, pendulous skin under his throat hypnotizing her into immobility. He took a step forward, then halted to stare at her. His large ears drooped along side his large head, accenting the menacing curve of his horns that curled above them like a demon's horns. But it was his eyes that held her, small and dark and not at all like the warm brown eyes she had always associated with cattle. No, these eyes were haughty and malevolent with their arrogantly sinister gleam. Coley felt the skin crawl up her back with her dawning comprehension.

This was Satan! The bull that had killed Rick and scarred Jason! The colour drained from her face as she stared at the bull with a mounting fear. A nightmare-like feeling washed over her of a desire to flee while her legs remained fixed on the bottom rail. Her mouth was dry as she watched the Brahma lower his head and make one incisive furrow in the sun-scorched earth with his large front hoof. She was too frightened to call out or to move. With an ever-growing terror she watched the signalling hoof ripping the earth in mounting fury.

Was this how Jase had felt? This terror that gripped the mind and body in a stranglehold that forbade them to move? Had he been able to swallow? Had Satan's evil hypnotism frozen him until the horror of Rick's screams broke the trance?

Her fingers tightened their hold on the fence, her knuckles growing white with the fierceness of their grip. Coley's breath came in short, panting sobs as her eyes watched with rounded horror the beginning movements of the bull's charge.

In the next instant she was ripped from the fence, the piercing scream of agonizing fear at last torn from her throat. Roughly her head was pushed against a solid chest where her voice was muffled by a dusty cotton shirt. The familiar scent of cigar smoke clinging to the fabric broke the hysterical cries. The rigid terror that had held her captive was gone and Coley collapsed in Jason's arms. She was safe. He had rescued her and the sobs of relief were welcomed.

The circle of his arms nearly crushed her as he held her ever tighter to him, but Coley didn't care. His own face was pressed against the top of her head and though he was speaking it was too muffled to understand. And then she was being slowly disentangled from his arms as Jase held her away from him. Her long fingers remained resting on his chest as she looked up into his face. It was as drained of colour as hers had been and there was no mask to hide the slowly receding anxiety in his eyes.

'I was so frightened I couldn't move,' Coley whispered as she leaned slightly towards him with a desire to return to the shelter of his arms.

'You should have been,' Jase replied huskily, giving her shoulders a sharp shake. 'You were told to stay away from here.'

Coley looked into his face now, her lips forming the words of explanation, but the icy cold anger in his eyes smothered the words. He had withdrawn from her, back behind his mask.

'Jase, please. Don't shut me out,' she pleaded softly, blinking quickly to hold back the tears.

It was as if he hadn't even heard her speak. 'I don't want to ever find you anywhere near these pens again,' he said coldly, releasing her shoulders to stand towering above her. 'There's an invisible line that runs from the house to the stables and I don't want to ever find you off that path. If I do, you can consider anything outside of the house yard off limits. Do you understand?'

'Yes,' Coley answered weakly. Her round eyes glanced away from the ice-blue hardness of his gaze. Just for a moment she thought he softened towards her and she added, 'I'm glad you're back.'

'Go up to the house,' Jase ordered sharply, and her shoulders sagged under the harshness of his tone.

Slowly she turned and took a few steps in the direction of the house. She hesitated and then looked over her shoulder, trembling under the censure in his cold, rigid expression.

'That was Satan, wasn't it?' she said quietly. The almost imperceptible distension of his nostrils answered her, although Jase didn't utter a word. He just eyed her coldly and turned away towards the pens.

It was a long walk to the house and though the distance shortened with each step, Coley felt each step she took was widening the distance between her and Jase. She spent a miserable evening in the house despite Danny and Tony's attempts to cheer her up. Later Danny came to her room, but she couldn't bring herself to confide in him. Somehow the simple incident seemed so complicated that she didn't know how to explain it to him without him scoffing at her overactive imagination, so she said nothing.

The next three days were equally miserable as Coley made the picket fence around the house her prison walls. She had no wish to incur Jason's wrath following that imaginary line to the stables. She tried to busy herself helping Aunt Willy in her rose garden and when that failed she would exhaust herself in the pool. But after sitting through the evening meal while Jase repeatedly ignored her and for the fourth time in a row excused himself from the table as soon as everyone was through to go heaven knew where, Coley felt she had reached the end of her tether. A restless despair consumed her as she sat on the porch with her Aunt Willy and Uncle Ben. From deep within the hills came the echoing rumbles of a distant storm, with faraway flashes of lightning.

'Looks like we'll have a summer storm on us before morning,' Aunt Willy said. 'I certainly hope it won't be too severe. The last one played havoc with my rose blooms. You seem very upset tonight, Colleen dear. Is anything wrong?'

'No, Aunt Willy,' she answered quickly. 'I was just thinking maybe I'd go up to my room, take a quiet bath and get an early night. My nerves are a little on edge—from the storm, I suppose.'

Gratefully for Coley, her aunt accepted the explanation and she sped up the steps and into her room before any more questions were asked that she couldn't answer. The bath did little to soothe her. In fact the stifling stillness of the coming storm made Coley wish she had showered instead of soaking in a tub of scented bubbles and hot water. Pulling the covers to the foot of her bed, she laid her robe on a chair before leaning back on the sticky sheets to stare at the ceiling.

A blinding flash of light followed immediately by an explosion of thunder wakened Coley from her fitful sleep. Her heart was beating at a frantic pace as she sat up in the bed and waited in fear for the last echo of the thunder to roll away. Another bolt of lightning flashed outside her window and she quickly covered her ears with her hands and squinched her eyes shut until the next roll of thunder passed. In the brief lull that followed she hopped from her bed, grabbing her robe as she went by the chair and out of her bedroom door. The darkness of the hallway stopped her as she fumbled for the light switch. Then her fingers stopped their search; she didn't want to waken the others. She groped in the darkness for the stair banister while the intermittent lightning eerily illuminated the interior of the darkened house.

Silently Coley inched down the stairway, flinching

at each reverberating roll of thunder. Downstairs at last, she tiptoed through the hall, one hand trailing to rest at her throat where it could immediately reach her mouth and stifle any cry she might make that would awake the rest of the house. The ominous darkness of the rooms beckoned her only to stop her with the sudden, blinding glare of lightning.

The rain had just begun, its rapid pitter-pat racing against the swift tempo of her pulse. Behind her, the grandfather clock chimed the first hour, frightening her with its unexpectedness. She stumbled against the little table in the hallway and valiantly chased after the rocking vase of flowers all the way to the floor where it smashed with unnatural loudness in the silence.

'Who's there?' came a booming voice from an adjacent room. 'Willy? Is that you?'

The soft whirr of turning wheels reached Coley just before the beam of a flashlight. With a little smile of relief, she swallowed her heart before turning with trembling legs towards her uncle.

'It's me, Uncle Ben,' she whispered softly, her voice still in tune with her shaking legs. 'I knocked over the vase.'

Obligingly, he shone the light down on to the scattered fragments as she swiftly gathered them up.

'What are you doing up?' he asked gruffly behind the glare of the flashlight.

'The storm woke me,' Coley replied, placing the broken pieces in the wastebasket.

'Frightened of them, huh?' Ben snorted, wheeling his chair around, leaving her in blackness. An ominous clap of thunder sent her scurrying after him. 'Couldn't sleep myself.'

Inside his den, the grey-haired man steered his

chair over to the curtains and closed them, shutting out the storm. Then wheeling his chair over to the desk, he laid the flashlight down and lit two candles.

'Electricity's out,' he explained, glancing briefly at Coley's white face before manoeuvring his wheelchair behind the desk. 'Sit down, girl. Might as well relax and talk to me until this storm blows over.'

She sat down in one of the larger cushioned chairs, although she couldn't relax, not amidst the rumblings of thunder that still echoed into the room. The flickering candlelight cast a softening glow on the leathery face across from her.

'My wife, rest her soul, used to pace from window to window every time there was a storm,' Ben mused, gazing reminiscently into the flame of the candle. In the wavering light, Coley saw the twinkle gleaming in his blue eyes as he glanced over at her. 'So I'm very accustomed to soothing frightened young women during a storm.'

'You miss her,' Coley said, smiling back at his twinkling eyes.

'Yes,' Ben sighed. 'She's been gone for—well, ten years now. Just shortly after our only child, our son, and his wife were killed in an auto crash, she died.' A glimmer of pain flickered briefly on his face. 'Willy's husband had passed on the year before, so she moved in with me. And the place hasn't been the same since.

'It's strange how the violence of a storm can bring back the good memories,' he went on absently, his voice a little husky and nostalgic. He opened a drawer of the desk and took out a gilt-edged frame. He touched the face of it fondly before handing it over to Coley. 'My wife,' he said in explanation. His tone was almost reverent as he spoke. 'That was taken a few

122

months before she died.'

It was a family portrait with the woman seated in the centre smiling sadly out at Coley. The slender, faintly lined neck was holding erect a proud white head, but the suffering expression in her eyes reached out to Coley as if to explain that the will to live was gone. The woman's delicate hand was gripping her husband's tightly, a more robust Ben Savage than was seated before Coley now. His hair was quite dark in the picture and there weren't as many lines on his tanned face. Then Coley was drawn to the two men standing on either side of the couple. One she easily recognized as Jase, his blue eyes warmly looking out at her. Naturally he looked much younger and the scar wasn't there, just the rugged good looks accented by the confident tilt of his head.

And the last person in the picture was Rick, a boyish laughing face barely concealing the mischievous twinkle in his eye. Coley recognized the resemblance to Jase, but Rick's face was softer not just because of lack of maturity either. No, it was the openness, the love-of-life expression that separated them. Yes, Coley could see how everyone would be drawn to Rick. Reluctantly she handed the picture back to Ben, wishing she could study it a little longer.

Ben cradled it gently in his two gnarled hands as he gazed at it fondly. His forehead furrowed slightly before he put it down on the desk.

'Tragedies always come in threes,' he said softly, staring down at the picture. 'I lost my grandson just five years ago.'

'I know,' Coley murmured. Ben glanced up at her sharply, his mind no longer drifting in memories but centred entirely on her. She squirmed uncomfortably

123

under his gaze. 'Tony told me.'

'And Jase,' Ben sneered, 'what did he tell you?'

'He ... he ... told me to ... to stay out of it,' Coley stammered as her hands nervously twirled with the tie of her robe.

'That's all?' Ben asked, and snorted when Coley nodded.

'But Uncle Ben, it was an accident. I'm sure it was an accident,' she hurried, her words spilling over themselves in the urgency of speaking before Ben did.

'You two have been together an awful lot lately,' Ben said, the hawklike sharpness inspecting the reddening of her cheeks. 'You aren't——'

'Of course not,' Coley interrupted, not wanting to hear how he might have ended the sentence. 'It's just that—well, I saw Satan the other day.' She leaned forward earnestly. 'And I was scared. I was so scared I couldn't move, I couldn't run, I couldn't scream. I couldn't do anything. Then Jase pulled me off the fence just before the bull charged.' The old man's eyes flickered ominously. 'So you see, Jase saved me.'

'But how long did he stand there just as terrified as you? And what part did Jase play in those scratches on your hands a few days ago?' Ben asked astutely, and Coley paled at his words. Then with an almost physical shake of his head, he seemed to throw off her words. 'The storm's died down. You'd better go up to bed.' As she opened her mouth to speak again, Ben raised his hand and she saw the weakness and tiredness etched vividly on his face. 'And take that advice he gave you—stay out of it. I'm too old a dog to be learning new tricks and he's like the leopard that can't change its spots. Go to bed.'

Glumly, feeling she had somehow failed both Uncle

Ben and Jase as well as herself, Coley accepted the flashlight and followed the beam out the door and into the hallway. She tiptoed up the stairs, grimacing at each betraying creak of the steps. She was almost to her room when she heard a door open beside her. She flashed the light on to Jason's face.

'What are you doing?' he asked.

'The electricity's out,' Coley whispered as he reached out and directed the light out of his eyes.

'I know that,' he answered softly. 'I meant what were you doing up?'

'The storm woke me.'

'I wondered if you would sleep through it,' said Jase, the reaching circle of the flashlight beam outlining a faint smile. 'Where have you been?'

'Downstairs,' Coley replied hesitantly. 'Uncle Ben was up, too, so I've been talking to him. Do you think the storm's over for the night?'

She asked the question quickly to stop the mask from stealing over his face, and succeeded. He said he thought it was. He took the flashlight from her hand and led her to her door. For the first time, Coley noticed he only had on a pair of trousers and she had to pass that broad expanse of naked chest to get to her room. Her heart beat wildly as she stared at the curly black cloud of hair on his chest and wondered absently what it would feel like to touch it. Then his arm was around her shoulders and pushing her into her room. As she turned back to him, he placed the flashlight in her hand, turning the light off as he did so.

'Good night, Coley,' he said firmly, and closed the door, shutting her in and him out.

CHAPTER SEVEN

COLEY lightly trailed her finger along the outer edge of a burgundy red rose, revelling in the velvety softness of its petals. She swatted absently at a buzzing insect harassing the bare legs beneath her shorts. Glancing briefly at her golden tan, she was reminded of Jason's comment that she was a 'long-stemmed yellow rose'. That seemed such a long time ago. Now he treated her with a brotherly indulgence and indifference. Not even brotherly, really, he never got that personal. All in all, she sighed deeply, since the night of the storm almost a week ago, their relationship, if that was what you could call it, had reached an impasse.

It was frustrating, she thought, positively frustrating. In the past when they were together, although it hadn't been altogether satisfactory, at least he had been interested in her. Now he seemed to have patted her on the head and said run along, like a good little girl. Like a child, Coley thought angrily, taking out her temper on the rose stem and getting pricked in the process by one of the thorns. At her unwitting yelp of pain, Aunt Willy turned just as Coley put her finger to her mouth to bite the wound.

'Coley, I told you to be careful of those thorns, they're so painful,' Aunt Willy remonstrated lightly.

The silver-haired woman dabbed her face daintily with an embroidered handkerchief, bumping her broad straw hat askew as she did so.

126

'I'm so glad we have those big oaks to shade my roses from the afternoon sun. They'd just shrivel up and dry away without them in this heat.' Aunt Willy took the roses from Coley's arms and put them in her basket before walking on to another group of bushes. 'It's so difficult to grow roses in the south-west because of the intensity of the sun—did you know that, Colleen?'

Without waiting for her to answer, Aunt Willy went on, enthralled by her very favourite subject.

'But if you really want to see roses, my dear, I mean thousands and thousands of roses, you must go to Tyler, Texas. More than half of this nation's field-grown roses are produced there. Most people think of oil and oil wells, when you mention Tyler, but they've been growing roses commercially in Tyler since the 1870s. It's a standing joke that if there's oil underneath a rosebush, the rose stays. I'm sure that's a bit of an exaggeration, but we Texans are prone to exaggerate.'

Aunt Willy laughed her tinkly laugh, but Coley knew that Aunt Willy secretly applauded the thought.

'They have over five hundred different varieties. And all colours, from the whitest white to reds so dark that you wouldn't be able to spot them if they were floating in a pool of oil. George took me there several times in October when they have their festival. You really must go there some time and walk through Tyler Park in downtown,' Aunt Willy urged with a wave of her shearers. 'It's an experience you'll never forget.'

Coley nodded absently, not able to mount much enthusiasm for the thought. She was too wrapped up in her dilemma over Jase to get excited about roses. That

127

dumb Savage pride ruined everything, she thought.

'You're very silent. Is there anything wrong?' Aunt Willy asked as she took her gaze off her beloved roses long enough to see the disgruntled expression on Coley's face.

'Oh, it's this ridiculous feud between Jase and Uncle Ben,' Coley grumbled.

'It's hardly ridiculous, my dear,' Aunt Willy replied, her eyebrows raised at the unexpected subject. 'There's a bit more to it than that.'

'I know what it's about,' Coley answered a little sharply. 'But Jase is Uncle Ben's grandson. He can't really believe that Jase would let his own brother die.'

'Fear does strange things to people, Colleen. In some people, their adrenalin increases to such a point that they're capable of doing things beyond the range of their normal strength. Others are turned to petrified stone. In one case we applaud and in the other, we condemn,' Aunt Willy observed, picking up her shearers to give her attention to a rosy pink bloom.

'I can't believe Jase is a coward any more than I can believe he's a murderer,' Coley retorted, stung by the sagelike yet depressing wisdom of her aunt's words.

'No one can really judge your inner person but God, Colleen,' Aunt Willy said quietly, holding the now clipped bloom in her gloved hand. 'Only the outward, visible act can be judged by man, with compassion hopefully, and Rick's death was ruled "death by misadventure".'

'Then why must Uncle Ben go on punishing Jase as if he'd done it with his own hand?' Coley cried.

'You mustn't get so worked up over this,' Aunt Willy began.

'But how can I not when two people I've grown to

love are...' Coley stopped, her cheeks flushed at her words and the scrutiny in her aunt's eyes.

'Listen, child, you shouldn't get too involved with Jas...'

'I am not a child,' Coley muttered angrily. Staring at her aunt with almost unnatural boldness, she added, 'I'm nineteen and I'll soon be twenty. I am not a child!'

Aunt Willy fell silent at her words, busying herself momentarily with her roses as if contemplating Coley's statement. Coley stood beside her, quietly wishing her anger had not made her words so sharp. She had no wish to offend her aunt. She was just tired of everyone putting her down. If only she was good at something, instead of so useless.

'What we really should do, Colleen,' said Aunt Willy, breaking into Coley's train of thought, 'is have that party I've been talking about. You can meet some young people, get involved with some of their activities.'

'So I won't have time to brood about Jase,' Coley thought to herself, and was instantly sorry for the injustice of it. Poor Aunt Willy was only trying to cheer her up and, even though she couldn't manage much enthusiasm, Coley at least managed a cheerful enough agreement that her aunt was convinced it was a good idea.

Coley had to admit, gazing at her reflection in the mirror, that when her aunt made a decision she carried it through with gusto. The very afternoon she had mentioned the party to Coley, Aunt Willy had begun calling the various families in the area and within two days had a long list of acceptances for her spur-of-the-moment party. Coley never realized her aunt could be so organized, because in the next two days she supervised not only the preparation of salads and desserts by Maggie, but also the placing of picnic tables and lights and all sorts of decorations around the sundeck by Danny and Tony. At the same time she scurried into town to pick out the accessories that she felt Coley needed to go with her yellow chiffon party dress. And with all that, the household never once seemed disrupted, a concession that Coley felt was for Uncle Ben.

And now the evening was here, Coley's reflection in the mirror told her. Her hair was freshly styled by the salon and her yellow gown was just as beautiful as she remembered.

The first car of arriving guests had slammed its doors just minutes earlier. Although she had one passing wish that Danny was still upstairs so that she could go down with him, Coley had no real anxiety at meeting so many strangers. A few months ago she would have been quaking at the thought. Still, she wasn't altogether excited about the party. It just didn't seem to matter somehow. As she smiled lightly at her reflection before leaving the room, her heart cast out one last wish that Jase would attend the party and not join in with Uncle Ben's declaration that he was going to shut himself in his room. Perhaps tonight, in these elegant clothes, Jase would see her as a woman....

'There you are, Colleen dear,' Aunt Willy trilled as Coley walked down the brick path towards the sundeck. 'My, you do look lovely tonight. Ethel, this is my niece, my great-niece actually, but let's not discuss ages now.' Aunt Willy laughed lightly as she drew Coley by the arm into the circle of people gathered around her. 'This is Ethel Merrick, one of my dearest friends, her husband Bob, and her two girls, Rachel and Roberta.'

Coley nodded pleasantly to the two warm, sun-weathered faces of the couple and smiled at the two dark-haired girls, one a little older than herself and the other a little younger. But the long whirl of introductions had just begun, as more and more people began arriving and her mind began swimming with strange faces and names. There were the Hamiltons with a boy named Howard and a girl named Brenda; and the Rasmussens with five children, John, Joe, Janet, Judd and Jean; the Petersons; the Simpsons; the Johnsons; the Masons; and then she stopped trying to remember. There was just too many.

Gradually, as fewer and fewer people arrived, the segregation into age groups began, slowly at first and then naturally until the families automatically split up as they arrived. Thanks to Danny and Tony, Coley found herself drawn into the circle of young adults and was soon laughing and talking with the rest of them. She was proud of the way Danny fitted in, as easily as he had made a place for himself on the ranch. One dark-haired girl that Coley couldn't remember being introduced to stared at her openly, which Coley thought in passing was rather rude, but she was too caught up in the infectious good nature of the crowd to wonder about it.

The dinner bell rang out wildly amidst the deafening chatter of voices, followed by the familiar 'Come and get it!' which began another mad confusion.

'I'll get your plate,' Tony said, touching Coley's arm lightly as he turned to leave.

'No, you won't, I will.' A blond-haired boy who

131

had been sitting across from Coley spoke up. She quickly tried to put a name with the face—Rex, Peter? No, that wasn't it.

'Hey, come on, Dick,' another boy cried. Dick, that was it, Coley thought. 'You're always grabbing the new birds. I'll get it!'

That was one of the Rasmussen boys, Coley thought with a gleam of satisfaction.

'You were getting my plate, remember, John Rasmussen?' a lively auburn-haired girl put in.

'Of course,' John replied, a little disgruntled and red-faced. 'But I can carry both of them.'

'And three plates for yourself as well?' the girl retorted wickedly.

Coley laughed with the others and John joined in very faintly himself. The three walked off towards the long table of food, still arguing over who was going to bring back Coley's plate.

Coley turned to the auburn-haired girl and smiled ruefully, 'They'll probably still be arguing on the way back and none of them will have my plate.'

'I doubt that,' the girl laughed. 'There's too many very willing hands around to take their place. Just you stay away from John. I try very hard to make everyone believe he's wearing my brand.'

'I hope I didn't do anything that...' Coley began, rather embarrassed.

'Of course not. All the guys are interested in any new girl that comes this way,' the girl replied with a bright smile. 'Especially the ones that look as great as you do. By the way, my name is Jill Saunders.'

'Mine's Coley—to my friends,' Coley replied, accepting the freckled hand that reached out for hers.

'Freckles, the curse of red hair,' the girl named Jill

grumbled. 'But it makes me different from most of you golden girls.'

At that moment the dark-haired girl who had earlier eyed Coley so oddly walked by again. She glanced at the two girls coldly. Unable to conceal her curiosity, Coley asked, 'Who is that?'

'That's Tanya Ford. I can't exactly figure out what she's doing here. There isn't really anyone here her age, except ... but there I go again, letting my catty tongue run away with me,' Jill said, shrugging lightly, but Coley noticed the hint of red in the girl's cheeks. As she saw the questioning look in Coley's eyes, she added reluctantly, 'You probably don't know it, but she dated Jason quite regularly before the accident. At least that's the way the gossip goes. I heard she dropped him when the scandal started flying, but I really don't know. It was before my time. Oh, here come the boys. Looks like Dick won out. Come and sit with us, Coley,' Jill invited as the two boys minus Tony walked up to them, their arms laden with plates and drinks.

Coley nodded agreement. She even managed to smile and laugh as they walked towards the tables, but her mind was racing back to finish one of Jill's earlier sentences—'There isn't anyone here her age except Jase.' And she used to date him, maybe she wanted to again. For some reason, Coley's heart took a nose dive at the thought. She was glad for the food, because as long as they were eating she didn't have to talk. Of course, the food rather stuck in her throat as it went down, but it was better than trying to hide the tremor she felt sure her voice would hold.

She began searching the faces at the various tables. Now she almost hoped that Jase hadn't come. Then she saw him, seated just a couple of tables from them.

He was frowning and it looked as if it was at her. The next moment he was nodding and smiling as if he had just seen her. A warm glow flooded over Coley as she smiled in return before turning back to her own little group.

Shortly after everyone finished eating, the young group began massing together again. Coley noted that her brother had attached himself to a rather quiet girl with long brown hair. She gazed at him so adoringly that Coley immediately admired the girl's taste. There was talk of games and movies and finally someone suggested dancing. Tony followed up the suggestion by going into the house for the stereo and records.

'What do you say we go and freshen up while the boys move the tables?' Jill suggested, already moving towards the house.

Several other girls joined them. Coley walked quietly beside Jill who was busy chatting with the other girls. She suddenly felt apart from them, a feeling of aloneness settling in on her. When they reached the house, she excused herself, saying her lipstick was in her room. She tripped lightly up the steps, waving brightly to the girls that she would be right down as they paraded into her aunt's bedroom which was serving as the ladies' boudoir for the evening. Reaching her room, she quickly touched up her lips with a dusty pink gloss before wandering idly over to her window to gaze into the darkening evening shadows at the gay party below.

A sudden flare of light drew her attention to the arbour. Jase was there. At first she thought he was alone. Then she saw another figure step out of the shadows. It was too dark to identify the other person, but the voluptuous silhouette very clearly outlined a female figure. Coley knew instinctively that it had to be Tanya Ford. There was a sickening sensation at the pit of her stomach as she watched the woman move seductively closer to Jase.

When his arms moved to close around Tanya, Coley turned swiftly from the window. Her lips trembled as she inhaled with a deep sobbing breath. She couldn't go back to the party, not yet. In a few minutes, the girls downstairs would be looking for her. She couldn't stay here. With a sudden decision, she dashed from her room and down the steps, pausing at the bottom to glance towards Willy's room where their gay laughter penetrated the walls. She started to hurry by, but was halted by Jason's name being spoken by one of the girls inside.

'I think he's handsome. Well, not really handsome, I suppose,' one girl was saying. 'More masculine. He positively oozes male.'

'What about his scar?' another exclaimed breathlessly.

'It gives me a rather primitive feeling,' the girl boasted airily.

'Not me,' another girl said. 'It makes me feel spooky. I keep thinking about his brother and how everybody said he killed him. He's always so aloof, looking at you the way he does with those eyes of his. He just freezes me.'

'I think it's rather exciting, and dangerous, too,' the first girl replied.

'Shush, girls, Coley will be coming down any minute. She'll hear you,' Jill interrupted quickly.

With that Coley hurried out the side door. Tanya wasn't the only one who found Jase attractive. She skirted the more travelled routes, going towards the

135

silent and unlit patio under the oak trees.

'On your way to à rendezvous already?' Jason's voice mocked out to her from the shadows.

'Of course not.' Startled by his sudden appearance, Coley couldn't keep the anger and hurt out of her voice. 'At least, not the way you mean.'

Her heart was beating rapidly now as he joined her in the shadows of the tree.

'I saw you from my window,' she added tautly as he failed to speak. 'You were over by the arbour then.'

'Uhuh,' he agreed. His gaze narrowed on her tense face. 'Enjoying your party? It's another first for you, isn't it?'

'Yes. Everyone is so nice. They don't make me feel like a stranger at all,' she replied, cursing inwardly her spasm of jealousy as she forced herself to look into his face as she leaned against a tree trunk.

'I'm glad—for you,' said Jase, standing silently before her for a moment before reaching his hand out towards her. 'I imagine that Aunt Willy will have my throat for this, but I'm afraid I stole one of her roses.'

Coley reached out and felt the velvety softness of rose petals in her hand. She moved it out to where the light filtered through the tree limbs to shine on the rose in her hand. It was a deep yellow rose in full bloom.

'A yellow rose for a yellow rose,' he said quietly.

'It's beautiful, Jase,' Coley whispered, blinking at the tears that were misting her eyes. She tried to banish the thought that Tanya had probably received an exotic red rose. 'Thank you.'

'Here,' he removed the flower from her trembling hands. 'I'll put it on for you.'

Gently he pulled the rose's stem through the rhinestone circlet pin that adorned her dress until the bloom rested firmly against her chest. When his task was done, he smiled down at her and moved away to light another cigar. He puffed briefly on it before turning back to her.

'You seemed to be having such a good time that I really didn't think you remembered I was around.' His voice was light. 'You seemed to have no end of admirers.'

'Neither do you,' Coley remarked flippantly, and at the quizzical raise of his eyebrow, she added, 'I overheard one of the girls talking about you just before I came out. She really thought you were something.'

'Really?' said Jase with a cynical twist to his question.

'Yes, really,' Coley said tartly. 'Now let me see, how was it she put it? Oh, yes, she said you were very masculine and made her feel rather primitive. She said you were dangerously exciting or something quite close to that.'

Jase laughed without mirth. 'Everyone's bound to be attractive to someone. I'd hate to have you consider me to be repulsive—which I already knew you didn't,' he added quickly before Coley could interrupt. 'I believe the dancing's started. I'm sure there are some young men over there who are anxious to partner you. You'd better run along.'

He looked down at the impish grin on her face and smiled ruefully.

'Don't tell me, I know,' he said with an amused resignation in his voice. 'You can't dance, right?' At the short negative shake of her head, he added, 'You want me to teach you. What if I told you I couldn't dance either?'

'Oh, but you must be able to, Jase, otherwise who will teach me?' Coley cried. At his sudden smile, she added, 'Besides, I want you to teach me.'

The faint strains of a ballad came lilting to them through the night air as Coley looked up at him expectantly. Jase moved slightly, a beam of light shining on to the troubled expression on his face, highlighting the jagged scar on his cheek.

'You're better off having Tony teach you,' he finally said sarcastically.

Coley didn't speak. She just stood in front of him, her round eyes blinking pleadingly up at him.

'Tell me what to do,' she begged when it looked as if it was going to turn into a staring contest.

Blithely she put her left hand on his shoulder and stepped close to him. Instinctively his right arm encircled her waist as the left took her other hand. His steps were simple and easy to follow and his hand on her back guided her movements until Coley felt as light as thistledown in his arms. Soon she ceased to concentrate on her feet as she realized fascinatedly that her head could rest quite snugly under his chin. Gradually there was no gap between them and their steps were mere shufflings of their feet as she finally laid her head against his chest and felt the gentle stirring of his breath on her hair. She no longer listened to the music, if it indeed was still playing. The rapid beating of her heart had long since closed out any melody the wind carried. His cheek brushed her hair as his arm tightened its hold around her waist.

His steps came to a stop while Coley swayed ever so slightly in his arms, her head lifting inquiringly up at him.

'I really don't think you need any more lessons,'

Jase said. His voice was husky but firm as he looked down at her.

Coley wanted to protest when his hands gripped her shoulders to move her away, but the thorns on her rose had caught on his coat, preventing them from separating without doing damage. Jase swore softly before reaching down to extricate himself. Coley took the time to study his bent head bathed in the light filtering through the trees. His straight black hair glimmered brightly in the light and his brows were dark furrows above cobwebby lashes resting against the tanned, square lines of his cheek. His aquiline nose shadowed the other side of his face, but she saw the slight distension of his nostrils that always marked a loss of control of his emotions. The green flecks in her hazel eyes sparkled brightly as she next studied the soft curve of his lips, so masculine and yet so desirable. From the corner of her eye she was half conscious that the flower was no longer entangled with his coat. His head raised and his mouth opened to speak, but no words came out as he stared down at her face, her eyes now raised to meet his.

Her hands slipped to his chest and then up around his neck as she moved ever nearer to his face, until the initiative was taken from her and Jase was pulling her to him, his head bending to meet hers. Their lips met, hesitantly at first, Coley's innocent and yet following her instinct and his restrained and exploring. A shiver quaked through her body, releasing a long-held torrent of emotion that soon engulfed her as Jase crushed her trembling frame against his. His kiss was no longer seeking, but taking and consuming. His mouth left hers for a moment, remaining suspended above hers until with a groan, he recaptured it, demandingly and hungrily aroused by her response. Then he was pushing her away from him, his arms trembling but his grip like steel.

Coley looked up at him, her rapture mirrored in her eyes. She loved him. She must have been in love with him all along. That was why she had instinctively trusted him. Why the slightest word could depress or delight her. She loved him.

'Stop it!' His brows constricted momentarily as he looked down at her.

Coley remained standing where he had placed her, just out of his arms, the fire he had started still glowing in her eyes. Jase turned away from her pleading expression, removed a cigar from his coat pocket and placed it between his lips, where he impatiently snapped a match to it.

'Dammit, Coley!' Jase swore angrily, staring out into the night's darkness.

'Jase, I . . .' she whispered.

'Don't say anything,' he interrupted, his voice sharp and bitter. 'Just go on back to the party.'

'I don't want to.'

'You forget, you're not my type.'

Coley inhaled sharply at his wounding words. Her face twisted briefly with pain before she retorted sharply, 'That's right, you like them more amply endowed—with a thick skin. Like Tanya's.'

'Yes, like Tanya's,' he asserted, gazing at her speculatively before the mask slipped into place. 'You know how to dance now and do a few other things,' he added cynically. 'Go on. You don't need to comfort the family's black sheep any more.'

'No, I don't suppose there's any reason to hang

around here, is there?' Coley agreed bitterly, with the barest hint of pleading hope in the last two words.

'Not unless you're the kind that gets a thrill out of being with someone whose name is just a little bit blackened, who's been accused of doing some evil deed. Perhaps you like to dance with danger. Is that it?' Jase asked scathingly. 'Tell me, that conversation you overheard tonight about me. You didn't say what they said about my brother. I don't suppose they mentioned his death at all, did they?' Coley blanched at his words, but didn't answer. Suddenly her face was caught by his hand and twisted fiercely up towards him. 'Did they?'

'Yes, they did,' she answered. The words were barely audible because of his tight grip. Tears began damming up her vision. 'It doesn't matter.'

'Ha!' Jase snorted a cynical laugh as he released his hold. 'It doesn't matter! You've got to be the most optimistic Pollyanna I've ever met. What do you think would happen if the two of us walked back to that party together?' When Coley managed a negative sideways movement of her head, he inhaled briefly on his cheroot before continuing bitterly, 'Well, let me tell you. The first thing that you would notice would be the silence. The second thing would be the eyes, all staring at us, shocked and condemning. Your brother would probably take me aside and demand to know my intentions and Aunt Willy would draw you aside to tut-tut to you about getting mixed up with me. If we were lucky, Ben wouldn't see us. Otherwise he'd probably raise out of his wheelchair to beat you personally for being so immoral, and he'd probably file a restraining order forbidding me to set foot on Savage land.'

The dam had burst and the tears were streaming down Coley's face now at the unbearable pain inside caused by the mocking contempt in his voice. Then anger seared through her as she trembled with rage.

'Savage land! Savage land!' Although her voice was low it vibrated loudly with her anger. 'That's the only part you'd care about. Savage land!' Contempt now laced her voice as she fairly spat out the words. 'I've never known anyone who could care about a bunch of dirt as much as you and your grandfather. You'd kill for this land!'

Jase towered over her, the blue icicles in his eyes freezing her with their intensity. His head was turned at just the right angle for the scar to be the only part of his face illuminated by the light. Coley cringed as the full horror of her words and their unspeakable cruelty dawned on her.

'I didn't mean it, Jase, I swear I di...' she began, but he interrupted.

'You were absolutely right. Good night, Colleen.' Finality was so clear in his words that Coley knew he might as well have said 'Good-bye.'

She stood silent, as immobile as the oak tree beside her, while Jase walked off into the darkness. A dry, hacking grief tore at her, knowing that nothing she could do or say would bring him back to her. There were no words she could call out to him that could erase the wretched words she had uttered.

Finally she picked up the rose that had fallen from his hand. The delicate petals were as torn and bruised as her own heart. He had once compared her with a yellow rose. He had even laughed about her thorns, but what did he think of them now? she wondered as a brief but hysterical laugh escaped her lips before she buried her head in her arms and leaned against the tree to cry. What had she done to him now?

CHAPTER EIGHT

A MONTH, a whole month since the party, Coley thought, staring at herself in the mirror. But it was as fresh in her mind as if it were last night. Somehow she had pulled herself together that night and returned to the party. There had been nowhere else to go and her absence would have been too noticeable.

Punishment for her hasty words had begun that night. The gay festivities and laughing voices had taken on a nightmarish quality as she endured it all in a stupor. None of it had seemed to touch her. She couldn't even summon an objection to Tony's persistent attention. Perhaps because she couldn't take her eyes off Jase and the dark-haired Tanya who clung to his arm, never taking her eyes off him either.

And now, a month later, Coley's torpor remained. But her reflection showed that this apathy had taken its toll in the dullness of her eyes, the drawnness around her mouth and the gradual loss of weight. Her appearance hadn't gone unnoticed. Aunt Willy clucked over her, trying to find out what was troubling her. Tony had become affronted by her continued lack of response to his attentions. Ben had been the most understanding, filling her days with busy but undemanding tasks. The hours spent with him had been the most rewarding for Coley. She felt in some unmeasurable way she was giving something back to him for the comfort he gave her.

Only Jase ignored the change in her. His subtle revenge was unique. He would ride off in the morning, as if on a day's work, and not return for two or three days. But his reappearance was always timed to coincide with Coley's presence with his grandfather, so that she could witness their maliciously cruel word-slinging matches. Only when Jase was absent was there ever a peaceful meal. Their bitter quarrelling and vicious jibes seemed to be the only conversation at the table.

It was as if there was no gentleness left in Jase. His face had turned to stone, the expression never changing, always cynical and mocking. His eyes were like an eagle's, harsh and piercing. Oh, yes, Coley thought, the name Savage suited him very well.

The burden of her guilt weighed heavily on her shoulders as she replaced the hairbrush on her dressing-table. At least last night she had shown Jase that he had won. It had been during the evening meal amidst one of their bitter arguments that Coley had finally lost control of her emotions. The heated dispute over some petty thing had driven her to the point where she couldn't take any more. She had dropped her silverware with a clatter and tipped over her chair in her frantic desire to get away. She remembered that she had stopped at the doorway, halted by Aunt Willy's imperious call, to look back at Jase. He had raised a quieting hand to Willy.

'But she didn't even ask to be excused,' Aunt Willy had protested.

Jase had given her a reproachful, silencing glance before turning back to Coley. He had stood there, looking arrogantly across the room with narrowed eyes. Then, with head bowed, Coley had raced out the door and up to her room, an ignominious exit but a desperate one.

Funny, when she looked in the mirror now she expected to see some starched matronly person instead of this youthful shell of a young woman looking back at her with haunted eyes. Cupid's arrow which had struck so swiftly had left an open wound in her heart. And despite everything, she still loved Jase. There was the cruelty of the whole situation, that those few brief words of anger to the man she now loved could destroy the fire that had flamed shortly between them. Her great hopes of bringing peace to the family had resulted in a full-fledged war. How many more battles were left before the end came? And how could there ever be a victory for either side?

Coley glanced at the alarm clock on her dressing-table. It was time for Uncle Ben's morning tea. Lately it had become a ritual for Coley to bring him his tea, a welcome ritual for her because it filled her morning. She had grown to like the dark panelled study, drawing comfort from its stern interior. No longer did she desire to throw wide the curtains and let the sunshine in. She revelled in the gloom just as she once revelled in the light.

There was no need to hurry as she made her way slowly out the room and down the steps. Maggie would have the tray prepared. Nothing was demanded of Coley except to carry it into her uncle's den, occasionally comment to about the weather, and, after an hour or so, return the tray to the kitchen. It was just as well, she thought to herself. Her wounds were too fresh and painful for her mind to dwell on anything but Jase.

She picked up the tray sitting on the kitchen

counter, nodded absently to the stern housekeeper and walked quietly towards the den. Entering the room without knocking, she placed the tray on the desk. She poured a cup for herself and Ben before settling herself in the huge leather armchair that cradled her deeper into the gloom.

'If these cattle prices hold, we'll have a real nice profit this year,' Ben commented, without taking his gaze from the books he was studying. When Coley failed to reply, his hawk-like eyes glanced at her above the steaming cup he brought to his lips. 'Well, aren't you going to say anything?'

'What?' Coley asked in a dazed voice before remembering just what he had said. 'Oh, yes, that will be great.'

'Your enthusiasm is overwhelming,' the man replied with a rueful shake of his iron-grey head. He peered at her intently beneath his unruly eyebrows. 'Not too long ago you would have made some comment giving credit to Jase. Have you finally learned some truth about that unscrupulous foreman of mine?'

'Uncle Ben, please!' Coley begged quietly, shifting uncomfortably in her chair at his deliberate lack of reference to Jase as his grandson. 'Your tea's going to get cold if you don't drink it.'

'Don't change the subject with me, young lady,' Ben growled. 'When I ask a question I expect an answer.'

'There's enough quarrelling around this house these days without you and me starting in.' Coley raised the cup to her lips to hide the trembling of her chin.

'What's the matter, child? Were you disillusioned into believing the sheep's clothing was real and there

147

wasn't a wolf inside?' the old man snorted. 'It's about time those ridiculous images of a knight in shining armour stopped drifting through your head and you saw Jason for what he is, an unspeakably cruel man who firmly believes the end justifies the means. But then, of course, he hasn't got the Slash S yet, has he?'

'That's rather like the pot calling the kettle black, isn't it?' Coley said bitterly, sitting her cup rather abruptly on the flat surface of the magazine table. 'Jase wasn't responsible for anyone's death. So what kind of a grandfather does that make you, when you can sit there and tell me that you believe your own flesh and blood would allow his brother to die?'

'So the thick skin isn't so very thick after all,' Ben said, leaning back in his wheelchair to allow Coley to see the satisfied smile on his face and the devilish gleam in his eyes. 'I'd almost decided you were a zombie, incapable of any emotion. But last night when you ran out of the dining room like the chicken being chased by a hatchet, I decided that maybe there was some life in the old girl yet.'

'This is the most sadistic family I've ever met!' Coley retorted. 'I've never known anyone who could get so much pleasure out of engaging in vicious quarrels.'

'Anger tends to loosen the tongue and let the truth flow out,' Ben snapped, wheeling his chair out from behind the desk.

'No,' Coley replied, shaking her head slowly. 'Anger is like a whip lashing out at old wounds to prevent them from healing.'

'Forgive and forget, that's your motto, huh?'

'If you can't forgive, you can't forget and vice

148

versa,' Coley replied with far more calmness than she felt.

'And that's what you expect of me, isn't it?' Ben demanded suddenly, bending forward in his chair to scowl at Coley. 'You expect me to forget that Jase stood by and let his own brother die because he knew that Rick would inherit this ranch, and now I'm to welcome him back into the fold with open arms.'

'But he didn't do that,' Coley cried, the hurt choking her breast.

'That's your heart speaking, not your head,' Uncle Ben mocked cynically.

'Yes, yes, it is!' Coley announced with a shrill cry, hopping agitatedly out of the chair to stand before him, her fists clenched in anger. 'I love him. I love him so much that I wouldn't care if he had killed his brother. I would marry him tomorrow if he'd have me. If I thought for one minute that I could take him away from here, I'd do it. But no, you've got him so weighed down with the guilt of his brother's death that he's sentenced himself to remaining in your prison. He could no more run away from you and your horrible accusation than you could if you were in his place. Instead he's condemned himself to staying here with a grandfather who loathes him, who never misses an opportunity to call him a murderer to his face. How severe a punishment do you require? That bull out there, that poor, dumb animal, took your one grandson's life and permanently scarred the other when he attempted to save his brother. And you're still busy extracting another pound of flesh. I think you're despicable and hateful, and I don't see how anyone, least of all Jase, could care what you think. If it wasn't for him, I wouldn't stay another minute in this house!'

'Stop it!' Ben shouted, his face red with anger. 'You don't even know what you're talking about. You weren't there the night Rick was killed. You didn't lie there holding him in your arms while his very life flowed out of him! How can you stand there and judge me when you don't even know what happened that night?'

'I know,' Coley asserted viciously, shaking with rage. 'I know. I had a very detailed account of what happened from Tony. He told me how Rick had gone into town and come home drunk. I know about how he used to play like a rodeo clown in the bull pens. But that night his bravado had come from a bottle and his reflexes were non-existent. It was Rick who caused his own death. Sure, his screams brought Jase, but where were the rest of you? Were you so firmly entrenched in your snug little bed that you didn't hear your own grandson? By the time Jase got there, the damage had probably already been done and the outcome a certainty. But did your cowardly, murdering Jase wait for reinforcements? No, he jumped into the pen and had his cheek ripped open for the effort. So don't tell me that I don't know what happened.'

Coley's anger blinded her from seeing Ben's white face with the tinge of blue around his lips, as he stared blankly up at her.

'But Rick said——' Ben's voice was faint and broken, 'he kept crying out for Jase not to stand there, begging him to help. He died crying out for Jase.'

'Of course, he would call out for him—after all, he was his brother, wasn't he?' Coley cried bitterly.

'But why?' Uncle Ben began. His face grew ghostly

150

white as he whispered, 'If it wasn't Jase, who was standing there?'

'I really don't know,' Coley answered sarcastically before turning away from him. 'It was probably a figment of his imagination.'

A convulsive jump from Ben's chair turned her attention back to him. Her hand leapt to her mouth as she stared horror-stricken at the white face of her unconscious uncle slumped in his chair.

'Uncle Ben,' she whispered, reaching out towards him, touching his arm hesitantly. 'Uncle Ben!' she screamed.

She realized he must have had a heart attack. 'I've got to get help,' she thought, and dashed madly out of the room calling frantically for Maggie and Aunt Willy. The housekeeper came flying out of the kitchen to meet Coley in the hallway where she managed to explain with very little lucidity what had happened. Maggie bustled back into the kitchen to the telephone extension, while Coley rushed back to the den.

Entering the room, she came to an abrupt halt. Ben wasn't in the wheelchair. It sat empty in front of her. A sound from the side of the room turned her horror-widened eyes from the chair. He was lying on the couch and Jase was standing over him beating his chest with his fist.

'Jase, no!' Coley screamed, rushing over to throw herself on his back and tug ineffectually at him. 'No, Jase, no! Don't kill him! Please, Jase, don't!'

With tears streaming down her cheeks, she pulled at his arm, but he shrugged her off.

'Coley, stop it!' he shouted, turning an angry and anxious face towards her. 'His heart stopped. I'm trying to save him!'

A trembling relief gripped her legs as she reached behind her for a chair to support her. How blind she was! Jase was attempting a heart massage and she had just accused him of trying to murder his grandfather! Finding the chair, she collapsed with a sob, to sit with tears frozen on her cheeks as she watched his desperate attempts to save his grandfather. What if Uncle Ben died? It would be her fault. Oh, why had she had to quarrel with him? Why hadn't she remembered he was an invalid? She bit her lip to prevent her growing hysteria from escaping.

'It's my fault, Jase,' she whispered, glancing beseechingly at the scarred face. 'He's going to die, and it's my fault.'

'Don't go getting hysterical on me,' he reprimanded sharply, not taking his eyes off his grandfather's face as he continued pounding on the unconscious body. 'Go and make sure the doctor's on his way.'

Her head jerked back as if he had slapped her. What had she expected, sympathy? After all the things she had said to him, why had she expected sympathy from Jase? With shaking legs, she stumbled out, meeting Aunt Willy who was rushing into the room. Coley's pleading eyes as she glanced at her aunt must have effectively foretold the gravity of the situation because the older woman hurried to the couch.

Coley wasn't needed. No one needed or wanted her. She continued her stumbling pace to her room, her vision obscured with tears, and flung herself on to the bed to sob out her shame.

She didn't know how long she had lain there when she heard the door of her room opening. Uncle Ben was dead. They were coming to tell her that Ben was dead. She shut her eyes tightly, then opened them slowly to turn her head towards the footsteps that had come to a halt by her bed. A very weary and drawn Jase looked down at her, his eyes blank and his scar standing out vividly against his tanned cheeks.

'He's dead, isn't he?' Coley cried, uttering the dreaded words for him. 'And I killed him, I killed him!' she finished, collapsing once again on to the bed in tears.

She felt the shifting of the mattress as he sat down beside her. She couldn't help cringing when she felt his hands grip her shoulders and pull her up to face him.

'He's going to make it, Coley,' Jase said quietly, but firmly. 'He's alive and he's going to make it.'

A lump of happiness gripped Coley's throat as the tears ceased to cloud her vision. She searched his face for the reasurances she needed. She bit her lower lip to swallow back the sob of happiness.

'Oh, Jase, if he had died,' Coley said brokenly, the horror fading away as the relief washed in, 'I could never have forgiven myself.'

'Don't think about it,' Jase instructed, brushing away a teardrop on her cheek.

'But it would have been my fault,' she insisted, attempting to explain the awful burden inside her. 'We were arguing and I was accusing him of terrible things, and that's ... that's when it happened.'

His eyes narrowed at her words and what little softness that had been in his face vanished.

'I don't imagine I have to ask what you were arguing about, do I?' he asked, rising from the bed as he spoke.

'It was about Rick,' Coley admitted very quietly, bowing her head as she did.

'How many times have you been told to stay out of that?' His face was turned away from her as he spoke, but Coley could hear the bitterness in his voice.

'I couldn't and I can't, Jase,' she stated. 'And you know why.'

'Well, you're going to have to.' His gaze turned to her face. 'Because the reason you thought you had doesn't exist.'

'I know,' she replied, lifting her trembling chin proudly as she looked back at him. 'I've destroyed with stupid angry words anything you might have felt for me. And this morning, my dumb inability to understand that you were trying to save Ben finished anything that might have remained. But that doesn't stop me from wanting to see you and your grandfather make peace. I don't think I'll ever be able to give that up.'

'Right now all I want you to concentrate on is making sure that Ben gets better,' Jase said, his expression unchanged by her words, as if they were raindrops washing down a brick wall. 'And so help me God, if I ever find you discussing me with him, I'll ...'

His threat was interrupted by a knocking on Coley's door. He glowered briefly at her before opening it. Danny was standing anxiously outside. He glanced at Coley before speaking to Jase.

'He wants to see you,' said Danny. With a hesitant glance at his sister, he added, 'and Coley, too.'

Jase grimly took Coley by the arm and escorted her down the stairs to the hallway where a bespectacled and harassed-looking man stood waiting.

'He isn't good, Jason,' the doctor said. 'I'd like to move him, but I think the journey would do him more harm than good. He's asking for you and the girl, but

I only want you to go in for a few minutes. If he begins to get agitated, I want you to leave immediately.'

'I thought...' Coley began. 'You said he was going to be all right.'

'I said he was alive,' Jase corrected icily. 'He'll make it. He's a Savage.'

'He doesn't seem to care whether he makes it or not.' The doctor glanced speculatively at Jase. 'I sincerely hope you *will* change his mind.'

It was a very frightened and subdued Coley who accompanied Jase into the den and Uncle Ben's adjoining bedroom. Her legs were shaking terribly as she came to a halt beside Jase at the edge of the bed where Ben lay, the upper half of his body distorted by a portable plastic oxygen tent that encased it. She watched the massive chest rise and fall in its shallow breathing before her eyes moved up to the pale face, the shaggy brows accenting the hollows under his closed eyes. The iron-grey hair looked strangely silver and ethereal against the snow-white pillow as the head turned towards them and the eyelids opened to reveal two dull blue dots.

'Coley, my child,' Ben whispered, a gnarled hand beckoning at her feebly to come closer and lessen his exertion of talking. 'You're not to blame yourself for what happened.' Coley nodded numbly, blinking valiantly to hold back the tears. 'No matter what happens, you're not to blame, do you hear?'

'Yes, Uncle Ben,' Coley answered hoarsely, and looked imploringly at Jase.

Ben was looking at him, too.

'I understand you saved my life,' he whispered.

'I had to, Ben,' Jase answered, his stone-like expression never changing. 'I didn't know if you'd

155

changed your will in my favour or not.'

'Jase!' Coley gasped, staring up into his cold face before glancing terrifiedly back at Ben. There was the briefest flicker of a smile on his face and his eyes sparkled brightly for a minute.

'You'll never own the Slash S,' Ben whispered. Then with a smile, he feebly waved a hand at the pair. 'Go away now. Let an old man die in peace.'

'You're too mean to die this easy, Ben,' Jase mocked.

Ben snorted slightly. 'We'll talk later, son. I need to rest now.'

'Yes, Ben,' Jase replied. His voice was sharp and clear in the otherwise silent room. 'We will talk later. I mean to have the Slash S.'

He didn't wait for a reply from the stricken man, but immediately turned Coley around and marched her out of the room. His hand maintained a firm grip on her arm, keeping her by his side as he spoke again to the doctor, all the time refusing to meet Coley's wide terrified eyes staring into his face. She didn't hear what was said; she didn't care what was said. Why hadn't Jase comforted his grandfather? Why had he persisted in taunting him there, Coley thought with a lump in her throat, there, quite possibly on his deathbed? She knew the attack had frightened Ben a great deal. It should have been the time for a reconciliation between the two, but instead Jase had made it another warring ground.

Her arm was released as his hand moved to her back and began guiding her towards the stairs and then up them to her room. Still she couldn't speak or protest. She was a pawn being moved about to suit the needs of her king. They entered her room where Jase quietly but firmly closed the door.

'Now, to get back to what we were talking about,' he said. His mouth was drawn into a grim line.

'Jase, why did you do that?' Now that he was no longer touching her, her mouth found the words to speak again. 'Why did you say those things to him?'

'Why do you think?' Jase asked angrily, blue-white fires in his eyes.

'I don't know why. That's what I'm asking you,' she retorted, hugging her arms about her in an attempt to ward off the chill his gaze was giving her. 'He would have forgiven you. If you would have just asked, he would have forgiven you!'

'Maybe I didn't want his forgiveness. Maybe I didn't want to be a part of some deathbed scene,' he said sharply. 'No, I won't be a part of some last-minute reconciliation so that an old man can go to his Maker with a clean slate, one that he couldn't have lived with if he was still alive the next day.'

'Fine! Stick that stupid old pride in the way if you want to,' Coley shouted, her voice trembling with her emotions. Only to have her breath taken away as Jase grabbed her and pulled her towards him in anger. 'Did you have to be so cruel to him, Jase?' she whispered. 'Did you have to tell him the only reason you saved him was because you wanted the ranch? Couldn't you have spared him that?'

'No!' His fingers dug hard into her shoulders as he seemed to control the urge to shake her. 'No! I had to make sure he lived. Hate can drive you on the same as love and if hating me can bring him back from the clutches of death, then let him hate me. Let him live on it and thrive and sleep on it, but let him do it alive!'

He let her go, the violence of his release almost throwing her on the bed, before he stalked from the room. Within a few seconds Danny rushed in, his youthful face drawn and pinched as he gazed at his sister with anxious eyes. She was still standing clutching the bedpost that had saved her from falling, the tears streaming unrestrained down an otherwise silent face. Seeing her brother, she reached up and wiped the tears off her face while she turned to walk to the window.

'What happened? What did he do?' Danny asked tensely.

'Nothing, Danny,' Coley answered hoarsely. 'It's me. It's what I've done ... to him and to Uncle Ben.'

'I don't understand.' Danny walked over to her side trying desperately to read the expression on her face, but there was none.

'No, I know you don't,' Coley replied, a little smile curving the corners of her mouth as if to show him that she was all right. 'If you don't mind, Danny, I'd like to be alone.'

Puzzled and still concerned, Danny gave in to her wishes and left his older sister alone in her room.

Within a week, Ben's condition had stabilized, as the doctor put it. In Coley's terms, it meant that he was out of danger and on the road to recovery, still weak but capable of blustering if the occasion demanded it. During that week, Jase had not so much as put one foot inside the invalid's door. Several times Coley had heard him asking Aunt Willy about Ben, but he never looked in for himself. And he usually had morning coffee with the nurse, an attractive woman in her late twenties. Yet never once did he ask Coley about Ben, even though he knew she spent a great deal of time with him, reading to him when he wanted her to, or just sitting and talking to him. Jase didn't value her opinion too highly, she decided. And she couldn't blame him. After all, hadn't she misjudged him often enough, once when he was physically trying to save Ben's life and again when he was trying to give him the will to live.

And Ben, he was too proud to ask for his grandson, but Coley could tell that he was expecting Jase to come and see him. It just tore at her heart the way his eyes would light up when the door to his bedroom opened and how that light would go out when someone else walked in. If only Jase would come to visit him, Coley felt sure everything would be all right.

Coley patted the neck of her horse Misty before shooing him out into the paddock area. The early morning ride had been a good idea in one way, she did feel a little refreshed. She meandered slowly to the house. The doctor usually came in the mornings and she was completely superfluous with the nurse there. At least the ride had given her something to do in between lunch and breakfast. In the afternoon she would sit with Ben and again for another hour or two in the evenings. In some small way she felt she was making up for bringing on the attack and being useful at the same time.

It was only mid-morning, but she would have plenty of time for a shower and change before she went down to help Aunt Willy and Maggie with lunch. The sound of her boots on the wooden veranda floor seemed too loud in the already hot and languid stillness. Coley opened the door to the house and noticed that Maggie had already gone around pulling curtains and shades where the sun beat mercilessly against the windows. The semi-gloom was almost refreshing after the brilliant Texas sun.

Farther down the hall came the echo of boots and the click of a door opening. Momentarily Coley hesitated at the bottom of the stairs. The doctor had probably come and gone already. Perhaps she should check to see how Ben was. She debated briefly, glancing down at her dusty boots and levis before deciding that she would look in on him, if only for a moment. She knew how aggravated and on edge he was after a visit from the doctor. Aunt Willy always spent the mornings in her garden and Maggie would be busy with lunch. Then she remembered the sound of footsteps in the passageway. Possibly someone was there with him now, but she'd look in, just to be sure. As quietly as she could, Coley walked down the hallway to Ben's room.

The door to his study was open and Coley walked in, glancing hesitantly at the half-opened door that led on to his bedroom. When she heard Ben's voice, Coley turned to leave. Someone was with him so there was no need for her to stay. Then she heard the other person speaking. It was Jase. Suddenly she had to know what they were saying and tiptoed towards the half-opened door.

'... All right, don't sit down,' came Uncle Ben's gruff voice, 'if it pleases you to tower over a sick old man.'

'You may be sick and you may be old, but you are a man, Ben, so don't seek sympathy with me,' Jase replied quietly. 'I thought I'd bring you up to date on the ranch.'

'Well, I don't want to talk about the ranch right

now. That surprises you, doesn't it?'

'Nothing surprises me.'

'I wanted to talk to you about Coley.' At Ben's words, Coley straightened, her body tensed as her mind raced trying to anticipate what he might be going to say about her.

'Coley?' Suspicion laced Jason's voice.

'Yes, Coley. She's fallen in love with you, you know?'

Her heart was beating so hard against her rib cage that she was sure its pounding could be heard in the other room.

'And you're wondering what my intentions towards her are?' Jase drawled. The indifference of his voice stabbed at Coley. 'Isn't that my own personal business?'

'It could be,' Ben replied mysteriously. 'What I'm more curious about is your feelings towards her.'

'Do you think I might be playing around with her?' Jase asked. 'Let me assure you that I'm not. When she first came here, she was extremely shy and very young. She's matured a great deal.'

There was a pause as Ben evidently waited for Jase to continue. 'I believe you're attracted to her,' Ben declared finally. 'Have you ever considered marrying her?'

'I've played along with your game long enough. Before I answer any more of your questions, I think you'd better tell me what all this is leading to,' Jase replied sharply.

Coley could hear the rustle of papers followed by a short silence.

'This is a deed to the Slash S made out to me,' Jase finally spoke, his voice deceptively quiet and ominous.

161

'I think you'd better start explaining.'

'It's really quite simple. If you marry Coley, the ranch is yours. All it requires is my signature on the bottom and Willy's and Maggie's as witnesses.'

Coley bit down hard on her lip to keep from crying out. The humiliating discovery that she was being dangled in front of Jase as another pound of flesh that must be extracted from him before he could earn his forgiveness was choking at her throat.

'Why?' Jason's cold voice penetrated icily into the adjoining room.

Coley's eyes were clenched tightly shut, the tears forming tiny drops on her lashes before cascading down her cheeks.

'Why?' Ben echoed. 'I would presume because you want the ranch. Hopefully you might also feel some affection towards her. Arranged marriages usually work out better if there is.'

'That's not what I mean. Besides, she's too young,' Jase retorted with exasperation.

'She's a woman, make no mistake about that,' the older man replied. 'She might not be as filled out as some, but her feelings are as adult as they come.'

'You haven't answered my question yet, Ben. Why are you doing this?'

'I've grown quite attached to Coley these past weeks,' Ben replied, his voice gruff and a little defensive. 'I'd like to see her get what she wants. She's a scrappy little fighter and I like that. For some reason, lord only knows why, she wants you. And since it's within my power to see that she gets what she wants, I'm doing it.'

'Oh, Uncle Ben,' Coley moaned silently. 'Please don't do this. Please don't make the ranch a prize for

Jase!'

'She need never know,' Ben spoke quickly to cover the growing silence. 'I'd never tell her, and you certainly wouldn't.'

'No, I wouldn't,' Jase agreed quietly as Coley stumbled out of the adjoining room into the hallway, her vision blinded by her tears.

She groped her way down the hall, until she finally leaned against the grandfather clock near the base of the stairs for support. She rested there, her mind racing with distorted thoughts. How often she had wished to find a way to stop the feuding between grandfather and grandson, and now she was to be the instrument to accomplish it. The pain tore at her chest. What a horrible and ironical twist of fate that one man would extract his last attempt at revenge under the belief that he would be making another happy and the second man to accept the offer to get the ranch he always wanted, while she, Coley, would achieve the two things she had always wanted—to have peace in the family and to be Jason's wife. Yet what a price they were all three paying. A transference from Hell to Hades?

She had no idea how long she had stood there, her mind flitting from one thought to another in rhythm with the ticking clock. Suddenly she realized that anyone could walk into the hall and find her standing there. Her state of mind was too confused and too hurt to attempt to explain to anyone what she was doing there or the conversation she had overheard. Quickly she hurried up the steps towards her room, but not before she heard footsteps in the hallway below her and Jason's voice calling out for Maggie and Aunt Willy to come to Ben's room.

CHAPTER NINE

NEVER had Coley thought she could feel so bitter.
When finally the humiliation and pain had receded
and the tears had stopped flowing, an overwhelming,
cynical bitterness had taken hold. Suddenly she felt
sorry for herself—for all the things she had missed
during her school years, of the times she had to stay
home to nurse her mother and of her great depen-
dency on others that had brought her to this ranch in
the first place. She hated the world—the world that
would twist people's lives until they were caught up in
a web of deceit and greed. But most of all, she hated
the burning desire within herself to hurt as she had
been hurt. Yet it was there, a burning, living thing,
smouldering in the green fire of her eyes as she made
her way down the stairs for the evening meal.

She had pleaded a headache at lunch time and remained closeted in her room the entire afternoon.
Even now the throbbing at her temples admitted that
her excuse was only the smallest of a white lie. And
the strain of the morning's eavesdropping was visible
in her fever-bright eyes and pale complexion. No, no
one would question the validity of her excuse as she
entered the dining room.

'There you are, my dear,' Aunt Willy spoke shrilly,
hurrying to Coley's side to inquire solicitously after
her headache. 'I was afraid that you might want a tray
sent up to you.'

'No, it's much better this evening,' Coley murmured quietly, half choking on her words as she saw Jase seated at the head of the table, the place usually occupied by Ben. 'How appropriate,' she thought cynically.

'I think I got a little too much sun this morning,' she added hurriedly, occupying Danny's chair to avoid being placed at her usual seat which would now put her on Jason's left.

Ben was seated in his wheelchair at Jason's right, his bushy eyebrows drawn together into an iron-grey line as he gazed at Coley, demanding of her to acknowledge by word the change in seating between himself and his grandson. But she couldn't bring herself to give him that satisfaction, nor could she meet Jason's glance that was resting so grimly on her face for fear that he would see the pain and bitterness that was lurking in the depths of her hazel eyes. Instead she smiled at her aunt and asked about her roses, knowing full well it would start a monologue that would cover any conversation for the next few minutes at least.

She couldn't have said what was served that evening. She tasted none of it, merely placed it in her mouth and nodded agreement to whatever her aunt was saying. Out of the corner of her eye Coley could see Ben fidget once or twice, glancing at Jase as he did so, but luckily, as far as Coley was concerned, Danny blocked her view of Jase and vice versa, so she didn't actually see what method he used in shushing his grandfather. Then the main course was over, Maggie had removed the plates and was bringing in the dessert. At that point a very impatient-sounding Ben interrupted Aunt Willy's dissertation on an especially hard to control fungus that had attacked one of her plants.

'We'll be having our dessert on the porch, Maggie,' Ben announced. 'And bring some of that wine, too. It's time we did a little celebrating around here.'

Coley's heart skipped a beat at his words. Suddenly she knew she couldn't bear to be there when he made his announcement that he was turning the ranch over to Jase. She knew she didn't want to hear the hypocrisy of his words as he toasted the new owner.

'If you'll excuse me,' she said, rising abruptly from the table. Her voice had a little catch in it as she spoke, betraying the thin edge her nerves rested on. 'I think I'd like some fresh air. I'll join you later.'

Her retreat into the hallway was followed by an angry exclamation from Ben, but Coley hurried through the door on to the veranda and farther out on to the lawn before anyone could call her back. Instinctively she sought refuge among the giant oaks that shaded the house from the purple-pink rays of the setting sun. She wished she had chosen something other than the brightly flowered yellow and orange sundress to wear this evening, but, at the time, she had needed the gaily coloured dress to boost her confidence.

She leaned back against one of the huge trunks and closed her eyes as the irony of the situation rained once again upon her. How she was paying for all those times she had misjudged Jase! Now was the time when her pound of flesh must be paid, but oh, was it fair that the pound of flesh was her heart? Was she a martyr to accept her fate so easily? No, the bitterness within her replied. No, she must make Jase feel the hurt and disappointment that she felt. Opening her eyes, Coley knew she would not make his victory an easy one. She would not be the instrument that would give the Slash S to him.

She heard his footsteps as he approached. She knew he would come looking for her. How else could he live up to the terms of his agreement with his grandfather unless he did see her alone? Perhaps that hidden knowledge was what had led her to leave the table so abruptly. She knew he would have to seek her out and she had made him do it on her terms.

'There you are,' said Jase, walking under the big oak tree to stand beside her. 'Why did you leave the table so suddenly tonight?'

'I was restless . . . and I needed the air,' Coley replied abruptly, moving out of the shadows and away from him.

She jumped slightly as he laid a hand on her shoulder.

'Coley, I want to talk to you,' he spoke firmly, causing her to clench her jaws to keep the pain in her heart from voicing itself.

'Please, we really don't have anything to talk about,' she replied, shrugging her shoulder to remove his hand.

'We've all been under a strain this past week.' His tone was sharp as if he was controlling his temper. 'Something happened today that you might be interested in.'

Coley ignored him completely and stepped out from under the tree and began walking through the waning light into the rose garden. She knew she was deliberately antagonizing him, but she didn't care. He was going to propose all right, but she was going to make it exceedingly difficult for him. She never realized how much she wanted to hurt him the way she had been hurt. She heard his quick steps as Jase overtook her. A malicious sparkle gleamed in her eyes as she realized how she was trying his patience.

'It looks as if we're going to have a full moon tonight.' But his eyes were studying Coley's face.

'Yes, it does, doesn't it?' she agreed, looking up into the darkening heavens at the pale moon. 'It looks rather sickly. It hardly makes one feel romantic.'

The light edge of sarcasm in her voice penetrated her airy words as he seized her arm roughly and pulled her around to face him.

'What's the matter with you, Coley?' he asked sharply. 'Why are you so bitter?'

'I should think you'd be amused. Surely the mark of supreme adulation is when the pupil mimics her teacher. I had a very good teacher,' Coley replied, staring into his face boldly, while allowing one corner of her mouth to curl as she spoke.

Even though her own heart was breaking into little bits, she could still derive pleasure watching the angry scowl cross his face as his fingers dug into her shoulders. How upsetting for him that she wasn't falling into his arms as she was supposed to!

'Come now, Jase. The cat got your tongue?' she asked mockingly as he continued staring angrily into her face.

'I could shake you till your teeth rattled!' His hold relaxed ever so slightly. 'What kind of game are you playing? Or do you want me to throw you over my knee and spank you? You're acting like a child!'

'But, Jase, you've told me repeatedly that I am a child.' Coley attempted to turn out of his arms, but was brought up sharply as he twisted her back towards him.

'No more games, Coley. Out with it.' His eyes blazed with their blue fires while his mouth was drawn into a grim and forbidding line.

'Don't you want to tell me how much you love and adore me and how you can hardly wait to marry me?' Coley asked in a mock pout. Her eyes flashed flecks of green as she spoke. 'I was so looking forward to that part.'

'What are you talking about?' His voice only thinly veiled the growing anger as his chest rose and fell at a rapid beat. His eyes narrowed. 'Where were you this morning?'

'Oh, come now, Jase. The night is young and the scent of roses is very heavy tonight. Surely you can think of more romantic questions than that.' Coley waved her hand airily at the night.

'How much did you hear?'

'Don't tell me I'm going to have to be the teacher tonight,' she mocked, curling her long arms around his neck and inching in closer to him as she raised her face to his.

Her lips touched his lightly and coolly, while her heart begged for one more minute in his embrace. The hands on her shoulders started to push her away and then dropped convulsively around her waist to draw her violently into his arms. She was crushed against his body, every curve melting and moulding to his, until there seemed to be no longer two bodies but one. His mouth punished, humiliated, consumed and ravaged hers until there was only one ruling emotion in her, that of passionate, yielding love. Then he was releasing her, disentangling her hands from around his neck, setting her away from him as if the fire that had consumed her hadn't even touched him.

169

For a moment her heart throbbed painfully, aching to feel his touch again, weakly submitting to anything that would bring it back under his spell, but that was before Coley's senses stopped reeling and her mind could once again rule. With difficulty she assumed a calm expression.

'That's how it's done,' she mocked. 'Now it's time for the pretty speeches.' He would never know the pain those words were causing her.

'I don't think there's any need for speeches,' Jase said, gazing down at her face indifferently. 'You seem to have overheard at least a portion of a private conversation with Ben. I think it's only a matter of "yes" or "no" on your part. Although I would like an explanation of your bitterness.'

'A simple "yes" or "no"!' Coley lashed out angrily. 'Oh, what an egotist you are! Am I just a pawn for you and your grandfather to move around the board at your leisure? Considering it's the rest of my life that we're talking about, I believe I have some say in the matter. And I say that I won't be the instrument that gives you title to this ranch. I refuse to be dangled above your head with a marriage licence in my hand and a little note pinned on me that says "Marry this girl and the ranch is yours". Strange as it sounds coming from a poor relative, I will not marry anyone without love.'

'And love would not enter into a marriage between you and me,' Jase said coldly.

'It most certainly would not,' Coley said angrily and with what little dignity she could muster. 'I know Uncle Ben told you that I was in love with you, but that wasn't what I told him. I said I loved you, but then I also love Uncle Ben, Aunt Willy and even

Tony, but I certainly wouldn't marry any of them either. Don't misunderstand me, Jase. I want to see you and Ben make peace. I know I've seemed to champion your cause a great deal, but Danny will tell you I'm a great one for rooting for the underdog.'

'You really lay it on the line, don't you?' His expression had never changed since he had released her from his embrace, and now he nonchalantly removed a cigar from his pocket and placed it between his lips. 'And those tempestuous love scenes of ours—I take it they're practice sessions, like the riding and swimming lessons?'

'As you put it so aptly before, they were experiments, lessons in human nature. If a person is going to learn, he might as well go to someone who has some experience, and you do have that,' Coley replied coolly. Her tingling body could attest to that. She glanced up at his rough hewn face. 'But desire doesn't last. Despite what you think, I'm old enough to know that.'

'You don't believe that this "desire" could grow into love?' Jase asked. His eyes studied her intently as he brought the match flame closer to the tip of his cheroot.

Coley held her breath for a second as her heart cried out the whispering hope that maybe he could grow to love her. Instead she replied coldly, 'I'm not about to sacrifice the rest of my life on the chance that maybe we would grow to love one another. Besides, if Uncle Ben has gone so far as to concede that he'll give you title to the ranch if you marry me, then you're only a step away from getting it without any strings. You might as well take that step, because I'll never consent to marrying you.'

'Suppose I told you that I already have title to the

ranch? That it was made over to me this morning?' Jase said, glancing at her sideways.

'On the condition that I accept your proposal tonight,' Coley finished with a superior tilt of her head.

He studied her quietly for a minute. 'Would you consider a temporary mock engagement? Until I can persuade Ben around to your way of thinking.'

'No,' she spoke quickly before the tempting idea could take hold. 'No, that wouldn't work at all.'

'So be it,' said Jase, dropping his cigar to the ground and crushing it out in the grass. 'You know he had his heart set on doing this for you.'

Coley glanced up quickly at his face hidden in the shadows of the night.

'I'll explain to him,' she said. 'He'll understand, I'm sure he will.'

'I wish I was half as sure as you are. He hasn't fully recovered from that last attack, despite the improvements he's made.' His voice drifted quietly to her, but the words seared deeply into her mind.

'How badly he wants the ranch,' she thought bitterly. So badly he was not above using this emotional blackmail to persuade her to fall in with his wishes.

'I don't care, Jase,' she spoke sharply, fighting the whirlpool he was sweeping her into. 'I will not be your fiancée under any circumstances.'

'I once accused you of being too sensitive.' His lips curled sardonically as he spoke. 'That drowned kitten I rescued from the rain has turned into a regular wildcat....'

'Please don't remind me of that awkward, gauche girl I once was,' she cried, hugging her long arms about her to ward off the shiver as she wished for the security of his arms.

He jerked her around to face him, his fierce grip cutting off the circulation in her arms.

'What happened to that girl who was more frightened of me than the storm? Where's the girl who was afraid of water, who was scared of the view from the top of a horse? Where did she go?' he demanded, shaking her as he spoke.

'She was too shy and too frightened to ever oppose you. But she grew up,' Coley shouted. 'Did you expect her to remain immune to the hate and bitterness and greed that lives on this ranch? Well, I hate now. I hate the way I'm being used by the two of you and I'm bitter that the trust I placed in both of you has been so abused. But most important, Jase, I've become greedy. I want to be wanted for myself, not for some dowry I might bring into a marriage.' She was trembling from the violence behind her words as she glared up at him. 'You didn't really believe I could stay the same as I was that first night?'

'No,' he replied, the word coming through tightly pressed lips. 'I did think you would avoid the conclusion-jumping crowd that abounds here.' Slowly his fingers uncurled around her arm until she was standing freely in front of him. 'You have everything neatly pigeonholed and labelled, don't you? But labels and pigeonholes aren't for people, Coley. You can't shrug them off that easily. Think hard on what's been said tonight. Later you'll be apologizing to me.' His expression was mockingly smug as he gazed down at her.

'If you think for one minute that I'm going to come crawling to you to apologize...' Coley began, enraged by his calm statement.

'Don't say any more that you might regret,' he interrupted. The light of anger shone through the window of his eyes before the shutters were drawn again. 'I'll be going back to the house now—to do some celebrating with Ben. I don't think you're in a very festive mood, so I won't ask you to join us. Good night, Coley, and pleasant dreams,' he added with a mocking lilt to his voice before nodding arrogantly towards her and striding off into the darkness.

She stamped her foot as she glowered at the retreating figure. She had wanted to spite him, to hurt him as she had been hurt. The bitterness had demanded it, and now even that was denied her. He had walked away, so arrogantly sure that she would be running after him to apologize. Never, never as long as she lived, no matter how much she loved him would she beg her forgiveness from him for the things she had said tonight.

'Coley, what are you doing out here?' Danny's voice called out to her. 'Jase just told me you wouldn't be coming in to join the party.'

'That's right,' Coley replied in a tight little voice that threatened to betray her emotional state.

'But you of all people should be there.' His forehead was creased by a frown as he studied her with puzzled eyes.

'That is exactly why I'm not there.' Her voice trembled with the vehemence behind her statement.

'Coley, I just don't understand you any more.' Danny shook his head as his gaze tried to fathom his bewildering sister. 'Since the first day we arrived, you've been fighting for Jase's rights, defending him. And tonight, when Uncle Ben has finally given in, you're out here pouting like a child that's had its favourite toy taken away from him.'

'You don't know the whole story, Danny,' Coley

174

began, the hurt choking her throat from the censure in her brother's words.

'And you have no intention of enlightening me either,' Danny interrupted impatiently. 'You've been acting peculiar all evening. What ridiculous notion have you got into your head this time?'

'You can stop the big brother act. I don't need one any more.' Her lower lip trembled while her breath came with a quickened pace as she fought to hold back the silent sobs.

His eyes mirrored the hurt and anger that surfaced at her words.

'I think you need a swift kick in an appropriate place!'

'Danny!' Coley called out sharply as he turned away towards the house. 'Danny, I'm sorry. I didn't mean to hurt you.'

He hesitated a moment before turning back to face her.

'No, I don't imagine you did.' His eyes narrowed as he studied her. 'But you're right. You're a big girl now. It's time you started working out your own problems without leaning on someone else. Whatever you've got yourself into, you're going to have to get yourself out on your own. Good night.'

She gulped down her tears while she watched him walk back towards the house. She knew what she was doing. Of course she did!

The steady drumming of rain on her windowpane greeted Coley as she woke from a restless night's sleep. The dark, sunless morning mirrored the depression that had hung over her head since yesterday morning. With stiff, listless movements she dragged herself from

175

beneath the covers, grimacing at the growling thunder that vibrated the glass in the windows. She grabbed a pair of levis from the drawer and with an unhurried motion pulled them over her legs up to her waist before reaching in another drawer for an ochre-coloured sweat-shirt. A very unglamorous combination, she thought, as she drew a careless brush through her hair, but then she didn't feel altogether too glamorous anyway. She glanced briefly at the jars and tubes of make-up lying on her bureau before shrugging at her reflection. Who cares? she thought, and ambled out of her room. Halfway down the hall, she passed the opened door leading into Tony's room. She stopped, surprised to see Tony inside with an open suitcase busily engaged in throwing clothes into it.

'Tony, what are you doing?' Coley asked in a dazed voice.

'You got eyes, Princess. Use them.' His voice was sharp as he continued piling clothes into the case without looking towards the door.

'You're leaving, aren't you? Where are you going? Why are you going?'

'Someone else now has control of the kingdom and the castle.' Tony walked over to the doorway, his thin face twisted with bitterness. 'I won't be sticking around to play knave any more.' His lips curled over his words as his slender fingers imprisoned her chin turning her frowning face up to his. 'You know, Coley, you not only have big eyes, you have a big mouth as well. Between you and Jase, you've finished me here at the ranch. I've got as much luck as my father had.'

'I don't know what you're talking about,' she murmured as Tony released her chin in distaste and walked back over to his bed to resume his packing.

'Go ahead, play your little games, but don't expect me to believe that you don't know about Uncle Ben's latest move.' At Coley's puzzled expression, Tony slammed the lid shut on the suitcase angrily. 'Oh, go on. Just get out of here. You've been a pain ever since you got here!'

Confused, she turned away from the door, hurt by the bitter contempt in Tony's voice as he ordered her from his room. The stairwell yawned before her and she made her way slowly down the steps. She hesitated briefly at the bottom. Breakfast waited in the dining room, but she wasn't hungry.

Coley slipped on to the porch, jamming her hands in the pockets of her jeans as she wandered along the wooden railing. A distant jagged bolt of lightning sent her retreating back to the safety of the house walls. She walked aimlessly along the L-shaped veranda, her desultory thoughts keeping her company, until she was halted by the echoing rap of a hand against a window. She glanced through the shadow-darkened glass to see Ben motioning insistently for her to come inside. Her mind raced to think of an excuse ... to no avail. So with a sigh, and a bowed head, she accepted the inevitable and re-entered the house, turning down the hallway to Ben's study.

'You're certainly a ray of sunshine this morning,' he scoffed at the sullen expression on Coley's face as she entered the room.

'It's not exactly sunshine weather outside,' she retorted quickly, sending him a withering glance.

'Seems to me I recall you were frightened of our thunderstorms. You were showing a lot of courage just now wandering out there on the porch.'

Coley glanced out the window at the dark, rolling clouds. Their angry forms seemed to mirror her own tossing and tumultuous emotions, her anger and bitterness mingled with tears of frustration and hurt.

'Maybe I was hoping the rain would wash some of this Savage dirt off of me,' she said sarcastically.

'Have you had breakfast yet?' Ben asked. At the negative shake of her head, he added, 'I thought not. An empty stomach usually sharpens the tongue as well as the appetite.'

'Surely you didn't call me in here to discuss my eating habits,' Coley said huffily, turning from the window to face him.

'Hardly,' he answered with an indignant snort. His bushy brows lowered over his eyes as he studied her intently. 'I was wondering why you didn't join the celebration last night.'

'It must have really been some celebration,' she replied with a bitter laugh. 'I just saw Tony upstairs, packing.'

'Don't change the subject on me, girl. I asked you a question.'

'Did it ever occur to you that I didn't think it deserved an answer?' Coley answered smartly. Then she noticed the knuckles on his hand, white from gripping the armrests on his wheelchair. The memory of their last argument came bursting through her bitterness and she sighed her defeat. 'I just didn't feel like celebrating the grand occasion.'

'But it's what you've been wanting all along.' A flicker of hurt and confusion gleamed briefly in his blue-grey eyes.

'When have I ever said I wanted you to buy me a husband?' Coley asked dejectedly, her chin trembling

178

as she fought to hold back the tears that threatened.

'I don't know what you're talking about,' Uncle Ben replied, a frown creasing his forehead. But Coley noticed the brief start of guilt that had preceded his answer.

'I went all through this last night with Jase, Uncle Ben, so it doesn't do any good to play innocent.' Her sad eyes gazed at him with pity. His misguided attempt to give her the man she loved had backfired. 'I'm not going to marry him.'

'You're not going to marry ... Did he propose to you last night?' The hawk-like look was back in his eyes.

'Not really,' Coley answered. Her chin straightened defiantly as she met his eyes. 'I didn't give him the opportunity.'

The funny half-smile on his face disturbed her, as if he was laughing to himself. 'You—uh—didn't give him a chance to explain things, huh?'

'There wasn't anything to explain.' Coley strove for an air of nonchalance that didn't match her nervous movements. 'He hinted that I should consider an engagement to ... to humour you. But I refused.'

'Naturally,' Ben replied smugly.

'You don't seem very upset,' she said, a confused frown creasing her forehead.

'Should I be?'

'Yes, I mean, I would have thought ... wasn't that the purpose of ...' She suddenly felt she was putting her foot in her mouth.

'I have the feeling that you were in my study yesterday morning. Am I right?' Coley nodded her head affirmatively at his question. 'I take it you heard part of a conversation between Jase and myself.' Again she nodded. His eyes crinkled at the corners as a short mirthful laugh escaped his lips. 'Oh, Coley, nothing good comes from listening to keyholes.'

'I'm certainly glad I did,' she replied, slightly angered by his laughter as well as confused. 'Oh, Uncle Ben, how could you have dangled the ranch as a present to Jase for marrying me? Didn't you think I had any pride?'

He tried desperately to keep the smile from his face with only slight success. 'I would say you have as much pride as any Savage on this ranch. As for dangling you as bait for Jase, I guess that was my final test of him.' His expression was sombre as he gazed abstractedly out the window before turning back to her. 'You should have stayed for the entire conversation. Then you would have heard him refuse the ranch under that condition, just as I would have done had it been me in his place. No, Coley, I signed the ranch over to him *with no strings attached*.' The last words were spoken clearly and concisely so that there was no misinterpretation.

She stood in horrified silence as the full meaning of the words sank in, before she collapsed into an arm chair.

'What have I done?' Her eyes filled with tears as she turned to Ben. 'The horrible things I said to him last night! Oh, Uncle Ben, what am I going to do? I love him so much!'

'The same thing I did yesterday, Coley,' he replied with a tender smile. 'Apologize and tell him what an old fool you've been. Except in your case, when you've been a young fool.'

A glimmer of hope rose in her as she remembered Jason's words the night before that she would be looking for him to apologize. 'Where is he?' she demanded hoarsely, swallowing the pride that had announced last night that she would never beg his forgiveness.

The old man blinked quickly at the tears in his own eyes and glanced out the window.

'Knowing Jase, in this kind of rain, I'd be out checking the washes for stray cattle in case of a flash flood.'

Coley leaped from her chair, her cheeks wet with tears, but her face glowing from an inner sunshine. As she dashed from the room, Ben wheeled as rapidly as he could after her shouting instructions.

'He'll probably be over in the eastern section near Blue Rock Mountain. Cut across the lower pasture,' he called as the screen door slammed behind the running girl. 'You should be wearing a raincoat!'

As he came to a stop in front of the screen, he chuckled to himself. She was in love. She wouldn't even notice it was raining. He pushed the door open and wheeled on to the porch. A few minutes later she came scurrying out of the barn leading a reluctant roan. Mounting quickly, she waved a hasty hand in Ben's direction before galloping off into the rain.

She raced across the flat pasture land, the tall grass giving her horse footing despite the torrential rain. The wind whipped her face, the raindrops stung her cheeks, but still she didn't check her pace. Then the land began to rise and dip as she reached the undulating foothills. Coley slowed Misty down, not wanting to risk laming her favourite mount as they began to climb the hills. Little rivulets of water were racing down and the sparse growth could not hold them back. In places, the ground was a sea of slippery, oozing mud just as it had been that first night she had met Jase.

She pulled Misty to a stop on the top of a ridge and searched the surrounding slopes and bottom land for a sign of him. A jagged bolt of lightning flashed brilliantly in front of them as Misty tossed her head and neighed her misgivings while the earth trembled beneath them from the accompanying roll of thunder. Coley patted the roan's neck reassuringly. She shivered slightly, her clothes soaked to her skin. For a minute she wondered how she would find him, then her eyes lit up with an idea. The lineshack! It was somewhere near here. Jase would stop there some time during the day. He was bound to.

She touched the roan's side with her heel urging the horse down the sloping ridge. The dry washes at the bottom of the slopes were filling with the run-off water. Even now Coley could visualize the water rising at the highway crossings. Farther and farther she and her mount rode, crossing hills, riding down canyons, until the highway loomed its shiny grey ribbon in front of them. She cantered Misty along the flatland until she reached the plateau that she had climbed on foot so long ago. Giving the horse free rein, she clutched the saddle horn tightly while the roan bounded up the steep slope, muscles straining with each slippery step, until they reached the top. Minutes later the lineshack loomed darkly against the morning's rolling thunder clouds. A thread of grey smoke mingled with the clouds and rain. With a shout of joy, Coley slapped her horse on the flank with her reins.

Huddled against the building under the overhanging roof stood the big red horse that Jase always rode. Coley dismounted quickly as she and Misty reached the building. Impatiently she tugged her horse under the roof with Jase's. Then she was off, racing around the building to the door, bursting inside with a shower of raindrops. Inside she stopped short, her happy eyes taking in the still form of Jase in the act of pouring himself a cup of coffee. Suddenly she was shy, frightened. What was she going to say? Where did she begin?

'What are you doing here?' Jase finally spoke, sitting the pot down and walking around the table towards her.

'I'm sorry. I was wrong. I was a fool.' Her words were rushing out of her mouth like an unloosed torrent of water. 'You've got to forgive me. I didn't mean all those horrible things I said. Forgive me, please forgive me.'

'You rode all the way up here to tell me that ... in this weather?' He gazed at her through half-closed eyes, his tone mocking.

'Of course! Don't you understand, Jase? Uncle Ben explained everything to me. You see, I only heard part of your conversation with him. I thought you'd made a bargain with him to marry me.' She struggled for the words that would make him understand. Her happiness evaporated with each passing second that he stood there so indifferently.

'And now that you know differently,' he said blandly, 'what am I supposed to do? Forgive you?'

'Yes,' Coley answered breathlessly. Her eyes looked beseechingly into his. 'I thought you wanted to marry me just to get the ranch, not because you cared for me.'

'You don't think that's the reason now?'

'No, I mean ... I don't know.' She felt so awkward

as she blinked at the tears that were forming in her eyes.

'I don't even remember proposing last night.'

'Well, I'm not asking you to now.' Her pride reasserted itself as the tears threatened to fall. 'I just wanted you to know I was sorry, that's all. You can go back to your Tanya.' She turned and fumbled with the door latch, the hurt, anger and humiliation frustrating her attempt to open it.

'Coley, I don't want Tanya.' Jase laughed, grabbing her arm and twisting her around to him.

'Let me go!' she shouted, twisting and turning as he took her in his arms.

Finally she was pinned against his chest with no more strength to resist. He determinedly lifted her chin with his hand until she was gazing sullenly into his face.

'Don't you see, Coley,' he said with a tender smile, 'you were unbearably cruel last night and stubborn, too. You never even gave me a chance to explain. But, darling, I love you so much I'd forgive you anything. I've never wanted Tanya, only you.'

Then he was bending his head, his lips touching hers gently, almost reverently, until Coley threw her arms around his neck to give his kiss back to him.

'Oh, Jase,' she sighed, minutes later as she pressed her head against his chest, 'tell me again that you love me.'

'I love you. That first night I had a feeling that you were going to change my life. I tried to stay away from you, to keep you from finding out how I felt, but you wouldn't let me,' he answered, pushing the wet curls away from her face with a trembling hand.

'I hated Uncle Ben so much when he offered you

the ranch if you married me. I knew how much you wanted this land. I didn't see how you could resist such a temptation.' Her face raised in glowing wonderment to his.

He touched her lips lightly before replying, 'I realized I loved you more. I loved you so much more that accepting his offer meant putting a price on that love, which would have only cheapened it.'

'Oh, Jase, what have I ever done to deserve you? I can't cook, I can't sew, I can't grow roses. I'm not even pretty.'

'Coley, you've brightened the days of an old man and filled a childless woman's heart with love. You give yourself, and I'll cherish you all the rest of my life.' The warmest light was shining out of Jason's eyes that Coley had ever seen.

'I hope all our children have blue eyes like yours,' she said before he covered her lips with a short but burning kiss. He hugged her closer to him as if afraid she would run away. 'Why did Uncle Ben change his mind?' she asked suddenly, pushing away from him to raise questioning eyes to his face.

'Because of you and that argument you had with him. You must have said something to him that made him think. At least, between that and a private conversation with Tony,' he answered, locking his hands behind her back to gaze down lovingly at her.

'I saw him packing this morning,' Coley remarked. 'But what has he got to do with it?'

'I didn't probe too deeply into the reasons, but I got the feeling that Ben has decided that Tony was there the night Rick died. The only thing that Ben would say was that he had judged too harshly and too suddenly once before and he wasn't going to do it again.'

'Do you mean that Tony was...' Coley began, only to be silenced by a hand covering her mouth. With surprising clarity, Tony's exclamation that day in the canyon came rushing back to her with new meaning. 'I was afraid something would happen to you, too.'

'Hush. Too many ill feelings have been nurtured by the past. I agree with Ben, there'll be no judging,' Jase said sternly. Then he smiled. 'Do you know you're drenched? And I am, too, now.' Coley shivered in affirmation of his statement. 'You'd better come over here and get some hot coffee in you. I'll get a blanket to put around you.'

Coley followed him to the table and accepted a cup from him, before succumbing to a giggle.

'What's so funny?' he asked, walking over to remove the blanket from the cot and put it around her shoulders.

She hugged it around her for a second before glancing up at him mischievously.

'I really don't know what good this blanket is going to do with all of these wet clothes on underneath,' she said innocently. 'The last time I was caught in the rain, there was a stranger who ordered me to take off all of my clothes.'

'Not this time, Coley,' Jase said, sweeping her, blanket and all, into his arms. His arms trembled about her as he gazed ardently down into her love-starred eyes. 'That would be demanding too much control even from a Savage.'

WELCOME TO

**The quintessential small town,
where everyone knows everybody else!**

Each book set in Tyler is a self-contained love story; together,
the twelve novels stitch the fabric of the community.

"The small town warmth and friendliness shine through."
Rendezvous

Join your friends in Tyler for the tenth book,
CROSSROADS by Marisa Carroll, available in December.

*Can Dr. Jeffrey Baron and nurse Cecelia Hayes discover
what's killing the residents of Worthington House?*

GREAT READING...GREAT SAVINGS...AND A
FABULOUS FREE GIFT!

With Tyler you can receive a fabulous gift, ABSOLUTELY FREE,
by collecting proofs-of-purchase found in each Tyler book.
And use our special Tyler coupons to save on your next
TYLER book purchase.

HARLEQUIN ROMANCE®

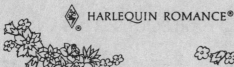

**Harlequin Romance
has love in
store for you!**

Don't miss next
month's title in

A WHOLESALE ARRANGEMENT
by Day Leclaire

THE BRIDE *needed* the Groom.
THE GROOM *wanted* the Bride.
BUT THE WEDDING was *more* than
a convenient solution!

Available this month in
The Bridal Collection
Only Make-Believe
by Bethany Campbell
Harlequin Romance #3230

HARLEQUIN ROMANCE®

After her father's heart attack, Stephanie Bloomfield comes home to Orchard Valley, Oregon, to be with him and with her sisters.

Orchard Valley

Steffie learns that many things have changed in her absence—but not her feelings for journalist Charles Tomaselli. He was the reason she left Orchard Valley. Now, three years later, will he give her a reason to stay?

"The Orchard Valley trilogy features three delightful, spirited sisters and a trio of equally fascinating men. The stories are rich with the romance, warmth of heart and humor readers expect, and invariably receive, from Debbie Macomber."

—Linda Lael Miller

Don't miss the Orchard Valley trilogy by Debbie Macomber:

VALERIE   Harlequin Romance #3232 (November 1992)
STEPHANIE   Harlequin Romance #3239 (December 1992)
NORAH   Harlequin Romance #3244 (January 1993)

Look for the special cover flash on each book!

Available wherever Harlequin books are sold.   ORC-2

HARLEQUIN®

Temptation®

the Fortune Boys

A funny, sexy miniseries from bestselling
author Elise Title!

LOSING THEIR HEARTS MEANT
LOSING THEIR FORTUNES....

If any of the four Fortune brothers were unfortunate enough to
wed, they'd be permanently divorced from the Fortune
millions—thanks to their father's last will and testament.

BUT CUPID HAD OTHER PLANS!
Meet Adam in #412 **ADAM & EVE** (Sept. 1992)
Meet Peter #416 **FOR THE LOVE OF PETE**
(Oct. 1992)
Meet Truman in #420 **TRUE LOVE** (Nov. 1992)
Meet Taylor in #424 **TAYLOR MADE** (Dec. 1992)

WATCH THESE FOUR MEN TRY TO WIN
AT LOVE AND NOT FORFEIT $$$

HARLEQUIN ROMANCE®

Some people have the spirit
of Christmas all year round...

People like Blake Connors
and Karin Palmer.

Meet them—and love them!—in
Eva Rutland's
ALWAYS CHRISTMAS.

Harlequin Romance #3240
Available in December wherever
Harlequin books are sold.   HRHX